UNEXPECTED JOURNEY

Where Death is only the Beginning

Diane,

Revelation 21:4

A novel by

Nicole Boddie

Nicole Boddie

THE UNEXPECTED JOURNEY

Unless otherwise identified, Scripture quotations are from the New King James Version of the Bible.

This novel is a work of fiction. Names, characters, places and incidents are either products of the author's imagination or used fictitiously. All character's are fictional, and any similarity to people living or dead is purely coincidental.

International Standard Book Number: 9781494967970

Printed in the United States of America

CONTENTS

Dedication

To

Marty, my brave husband, who encouraged me to follow my dreams, and never give up.

And to

All those who have found themselves in a hopeless situation. Know that there is always hope found in Christ Jesus.

1

GRANDVIEW NURSING HOME

Heavy rain pounded against Maggie's window. The crash of thunder penetrated her quiet and boring room. Very quickly, it seemed that the clear blue sky was overcome with ominous dark clouds. She could hear the note of each rain drop as it joined the larger symphony. After a few moments, the soggy clouds quickly dissipated, revealing that this precarious storm had passed. The only evidence, of that fierce afternoon rain, was a glistening sparkle coating the leaves.

Maggie watched the heavy clouds wring themselves out on hot, parched ground. Once the ground was satisfied; all those clouds simply moved on to water another patch of dry soil. Maggie enviously watched as beautiful mocking birds emerged from nearby sheltering oaks. Many birds sang songs with a renewed sense of excitement. After all, they were no longer grounded by hard rain.

"If only I could be so free to fly," Maggie thought as she stared out the window of Grandview Nursing Home. Looking at her adjustable bed she thought, "well flying is too much of a stretch, but if I could just walk again then maybe I'd sing too."

Maggie had lived a long life and suffered more than her share of hardship; besides that she was just plain, tired. Her eyes showcased the wear of tragedies that had relentlessly pursued her. Maggie often thought of all the loved ones she'd lost. Rendering herself helpless to past regret was painful, but memories were the only visitors she had left.

Maggie wondered if her whole life had been in vain. She definitely felt that the constant struggle to keep it all together was pointless. Her mind was constantly plagued with so many questions.

Maggie thought, "will I die all alone in this God forsaken purgatory, also known as Grandview Nursing Home?" Then wondered, "will people miss me, grieve my death or show up to claim my ashes?"

The longer Maggie remained captive to her bed, the harder it got to ward off fear and loneliness. Even an attempt at positive thinking proved to be unsuccessful. Finally, Maggie found a glimmer of hope in the color of nature through her window. She really enjoyed the spectacle of a rain shower, yet was equally impressed with its smell and sound.

Maggie watched the leaves as they were pelted by raindrops, which triggered fond memories of her life on the farm. Every day consisted of hard work, but her life was not complicated. A typical harvest depended heavily on a combination of hard work and a precise amount of rain. Some years produced such an abundant yield that the family was able to make needed repairs on their house or barn. Although, most years, after buying seed, there was barely enough money for basic necessities. Times were hard, but Maggie enjoyed doing her part to contribute to the family.

Their lean income hardly allowed for store-bought clothing. Forced to become creative, Maggie's mom usually made her outfits. Once a month Maggie accompanied her mother to the feed store. She was allowed to pick out the most recent hundred-pound bag of flour for a new church dress. Luckily, flour came in a fabric bag that was made of durable material. Each bag of flour had its own unique design printed on the fabric. Maggie was unsure of the packager's intent, but it worked out well for her dresses.

Unlike most families in the community, Maggie's parents' only had two children. Maggie's brother, Avery, was two years older than she. Having an older brother was nice because he often looked out for Maggie, and helped with all of her chores.

One year, Maggie talked Avery into helping her build a tree house. Maggie was delighted that her big brother wanted to help her. When the project was complete, their tree house was the most envied in the neighborhood. Due to Avery's skill in building forts and tree houses, he became the most popular kid in town.

As expected Maggie really looked up to Avery and followed him everywhere, that is until they got older. Suddenly, instead of being partners in crime they were now constant rivalries.

If Avery could scale the tree in two minutes flat, then Maggie would break his record by at least thirty seconds. Any activity was prone to competition. They often raced each other home from school, but skipping a rock across the surface of the lake further than Avery was Maggie's favorite sport.

Even a holiday such as Christmas was fair game. Avery would make a bet with Maggie that he could stay up later on Christmas Eve. Of course, Maggie usually lost, but all Avery ever wagered was the last Christmas cookie. Maggie and Avery grew up poor, which made for slim pickings around the tree, but Maggie's father really had a way of making Christmas fun.

Every year about a week before Christmas, Maggie's father would very dramatically run in the house.

He shouted, "Margaret, Margaret, when I was driving up the driveway something flew overhead!"

He continued, "It looked like a flying sleigh pulled by reindeers, and I think it was Santa making a practice run."

He paused, then went on, "He must be getting ready for next week."

He shouted, "Something spilled out of Santa's

sleigh after he flew over my truck; then made a hard right turn."

Playfully their mother would ask, "Really Charles, you saw something fly over your truck, are you sure it wasn't your imagination?"

In a matter of fact way their father answered, "I can actually prove it happened!"

She asked, "How can you prove it?"

Their father responded, "When old St. Nick made that hard right turn I saw something spill out of his sleigh, let's go outside and see what it was."

Their mother and father would run outside with both children in tow. Much to their surprise, something did spill out of Santa's sleigh. There were apples and oranges all over the front yard. It was just as much fun collecting the fruit as it was eating it.

Maggie's childhood was fun, and she was a happy little girl. When Maggie reached adolescence, however, she noticed that her mother was staying in bed a lot more.

This worried Maggie, so while out helping her father mend fences she asked, "What is wrong with Mom?"

Her father answered, "Well some people get sick in their body, and other people get sick in their mind."

Maggie asked, "Will she get better?"

Her father replied, "I'm afraid your mother will deal with this sadness off and on for the rest of her life."

Maggie wondered how and why her mother

got sick. She didn't press any further, because of the worry on her father's face. Whenever her mother would retreat to bed, Maggie did her best to pick up more slack around the house. At first, Maggie's mother isolated herself for only a week at a time, and three months in between. When Avery graduated high school and enlisted in the military, consequently, that sadness increased drastically.

Avery was gone, and her mother was spending most days in a dark bedroom. All house work, and field work now depended on Maggie and her father. This burden was beginning to put a strain on their family. Maggie had switched roles with her mother, and her father was growing tired of walking on egg shells.

Maggie was about to give up on having a normal teenage life, when she learned that a lady from church had a granddaughter who was coming to live with her. Ms. Harrison approached Maggie after Mass and introduced her granddaughter Priscilla. The girls became very close friends, and almost inseparable. July 31 was Maggie's sixteenth birthday.

Preparing for her birthday, that year, was bitter sweet. Maggie missed her brother, but at least a new found friend provided company for her loneliness. More important, Priscilla supplied an escape from an all consuming sadness that had enveloped Maggie's house.

That year for Maggie's party her mother happened to be on the upswing, and baked a cake. Avery couldn't make it home for Maggie's birthday, but he was sure to send her a present by mail.

She opened Avery's gift first; it was a picture he'd drawn of a cowboy. Maggie smiled as she thought back to her previous birthday. Avery had taken her to a picture show, and watched "High Noon". That western starring Gary Cooper and Grace Kelly was a turning point for Maggie, as she fell in love with cowboys.

The next gift was from her parents, her first store-bought dress! She couldn't believe it. Her mother must have been saving pennies for at least a year. It was so beautiful. Maggie was afraid to handle the dress, but her mother insisted that she go try it on.

She paraded down the stairs, and noticed that both of her parents were standing in the foyer with a look of admiration on their faces.

Holding back tears her father said, "My little girl is growing up."

Her mother smiled affectionately, and whispered, "You look so beautiful."

Maggie realized that she hadn't seen her mother smile, or her father so relaxed in months. That alone was the best birthday present ever.

Two weeks later, summer was just a distant memory, and school was back in session. Maggie hated the social aspect of school, but loved to learn. Kids picked on Maggie for various reasons. Those reasons were having red hair, being too smart, and having a temper! Maggie knew that she'd show those kids just how great she was one day, so she didn't sweat it.

Before she knew it Maggie's favorite season of the year had arrived. She loved everything about fall, how it smelled, looked, and sounded. Feeling a cool breeze flowing through her thick red hair, or watching the leaves glide down to their final resting place gave Maggie such joy. Her favorite thing about fall was pumpkin seeds, and the foliage change. Maggie often found herself overwhelmed with emotion, while contemplating colors so vibrant, and views so sharp in contrast. She felt connected to nature in the fall, because like that season she also displayed a unique quality.

The overpowering smell of fresh baked pumpkin pie interrupted Maggie's walk down memory lane. She realized that it was dark outside, and apparently dinner time. A new lady brought in Maggie's tray, and proceeded to feed her. Maggie could tell this lady was new, because there was something different about her. The new nurse's aide was a little more gentle in nature. She also seemed to invest more time in Maggie.

After Maggie was finished with dinner, the new aide cleaned her up by way of a sponge bath. After finishing her job, the nurse's aide left. Maggie didn't mind too much being alone especially after that last room mate had been so loud. That old lady talked loud, snored loud, and watched tv loud. Amazingly the old lady even died loud, so the silence was sort of refreshing.

The room was too quiet, consequently, Maggie's thoughts became much louder. In that stillness she was reminded of her very first loss in life. Maggie resented the power of loss, and how it had completely changed who she was. In fact, even the way she viewed her favorite season was altered forever. That loss represented a fork in the road, leading Maggie down the path of rugged terrain with plenty of suffering.

2

MAGGIE'S AWAKENING

Just as Maggie was settling in for the night, the mean old nurse walked in. She had a paper cup filled to the brim with pills of every color.

"It's time for happy pills," the mean old nurse sang.

Maggie despised all those pills; they were hard to swallow, and made her feel funny. So Maggie made sure to put up a good fight every time. Finally all pills were swallowed, and the nurse was satisfied with the outcome of her routine torture.

Maggie wondered if that nurse had given her the wrong pills, because she was wide awake, and thoughts were just racing one right after another.

She thought, "Maybe the old bitty's a sadomasochist, and keeping me awake all night to review my mistakes is an avenue of extreme torture!"

Maggie was afraid to dwell on the event that caused so much sorrow. However, the memory of that loss kept knocking from the door of her soul, refusing to be swept under the rug.

She thought, "Well maybe if I let this memory play out in full, then I can be rid of it."

Maggie finally gave in, and opened the door of a room deep within her soul. This locked room was where she had stuffed the most painful memories. As soon as door was wide open, those dreadful memories filled her mind. Maggie remembered that Friday well, after all, the following Monday was Halloween. School let out early that Friday for a long weekend. Maggie's parents were not crazy about what they considered the devil's night, and usually made her stay home. Maggie knew that if she was to get out, it had to be a celebration before the actual night of Halloween.

It so happened that the new girl in school was very wealthy, and announced that her parents were leaving town not to return until next week. The party would be that night at her house with plenty of alcohol, and a truck load of college boys. Maggie knew this was the opportunity she was looking for. Maggie talked Priscilla into sneaking out of her grandmother's house. It was settled, Maggie would stay the night at Priscilla's house, sneak out, and go to the party.

After Ms. Harrison fell asleep, Maggie and Priscilla escaped through the window of her bedroom. Maggie's heart was beating so fast that she thought it would explode. Terrified, Maggie held her breath until they made it to Priscilla's car.

Priscilla got in her car, put the gear in neutral, and whispered, "Push the car down the driveway."

Once they reached the road Priscilla said, "Okay Maggie, now get in."

Maggie ran around to the passenger side and jumped in with a sigh of relief. Priscilla started up her car and drove to the party. Although the place was packed when they arrived, Courtney, the new girl, spotted them. She brought Priscilla and Maggie each a drink.

With slurred speech Courtney said, "Be sure and get drunk!"

Maggie was too embarrassed to admit that the only alcohol she'd ever tasted was communion wine at mass. Trying not to seem inexperienced, Maggie guzzled her beer down faster than Priscilla. She soon realized that was clearly a mistake, because beer tasted horrible. It nearly came back up, but Maggie was a trooper and tried another beer. At the finish of Maggie's second glass, she was stumbling drunk. Maggie looked around, but Priscilla was no where to be found.

So Maggie managed to stagger onto Courtney's back patio, and caught the attention of the most striking boy there. He ran over to help Maggie sit in a patio chair before she fell, and introduced himself as Gator.

Maggie laughed out loud as she asked, "Who names their kid Gator?"

He said, "Well my name is Earl, but my buddies call me Gator!"

Maggie laughed even harder then asked, "Why?"

Confused, Gator answered, "Because I am the best alligator hunter in most of Southern Louisiana."

Gator brought more beer. Before Maggie realized what was going on, Priscilla was knocking on the window of Gator's truck.

Priscilla said, "Maggie, we have to go!"

Still not sure how she got into Gator's truck, Maggie got dressed. Gator wrote his phone number on a dirty napkin that he grabbed from his floorboard. On the way back to Priscilla's house Maggie threw up all over herself, and the dashboard. All Priscilla wanted to talk about was that guy Maggie met, and how cute he was. After they returned to Priscilla's house the girls crawled back in through the window, and Maggie passed smooth out.

The next morning Maggie didn't remember anything beyond the first beer. However, Maggie had a bad feeling that she'd regret the night before. Priscilla told her what she had witnessed in the cab of Gator's truck. Mortified, all Maggie wanted was to take a shower, and go home.

When Maggie got home her mother asked, "Did you have a good time with your friend?"

Maggie replied, "Not really, Priscilla's grandmother made us play bridge all night."

Maggie's mom smiled as she walked back into the laundry room.

Maggie went up to her room quickly. As she took off her coat, the dirty old napkin with Gator's name and phone number fell out. Maggie felt sick all over again. She crumbled up the dirty napkin, and stuck it under her mattress. Maggie tried to distract herself with a murder mystery book, but that feeling of dread never left.

Sunday morning brought its normal routine of going to mass; Maggie was not looking forward to being seen by anybody. Maggie wondered if it would be obvious that she had sinned. The whole hour of mass, Maggie could focus on nothing except the broken body of Christ hanging sorrowfully on a cross. The words of her mother rang in her head. Maggie's mother had harped on purity until marriage, and warned that in order to get a good husband she would need to offer her virginity.

Maggie's mother must have noticed her behavior was a little off and asked, "Is everything okay?"

Wide-eyed Maggie just nodded yes. She thought for sure now that she was going to hell, for the thing with Gator, and for lying to her mother in church!

After mass Maggie said, "Mom, I feel sick."

Her mother asked, "What's wrong?"

Maggie responded, "It must have been the beef stroganoff that Ms. Harrison cooked last night."

Her mother said, "When we get home, just go lay down for a while."

When they got home, Maggie was relieved to go to her room. Over the next few weeks Maggie was able to push out any thoughts of that dreadful night, until she noticed that her period was a full three weeks late. Maggie was terrified. In her mind she played out the different scenarios, and each one turned out horrible. Maggie knew her mother would be disappointed. She wondered if the news of possible pregnancy would send her mother back to a dark bedroom of depression. Maggie felt like a failure, and thought her mother would agree. Maggie knew she couldn't keep this a secret any longer, so she told her mother about Gator.

Her mother took the news very hard, but not as severely as Maggie expected.

Maggie's mom said, "There is still a chance that you're not pregnant, so lets just pray for that outcome."

The next day her mother brought Maggie to the doctor. The doctor collected a sample of urine and drew her blood. Without any affirmation of pregnancy she and her mother left. Once they got home, Maggie was instructed not to say anything to anyone until they knew the results. A week later the doctor's office called and asked Maggie to come back in. Maggie's nerves were shot by the time they got to the doctor's office, and signed in. The tension between Maggie and her mother was intense. A nurse walked into the waiting room, and called her back. As Maggie sat on the exam table, feeling more vulnerable than ever, the doctor announced that she was pregnant.

Maggie's mother dropped her purse to the floor, and yelled, "Excuse me?"

The doctor repeated the diagnoses. Her mother

looked at Maggie in disbelief. Then her mother's expression turned to anger. At this point, Maggie was very afraid. Maggie was instructed to stay in the exam room, while the doctor spoke to her mother in the hall. Maggie overheard them discussing options regarding her pregnancy. Her mother and doctor reentered the room, but neither of them looked at Maggie. Her mother simply motioned that they were leaving.

The ride home was completely silent. She wondered how her father would react when he got home, and found out. Maggie frantically thought about possible solutions to her problem, and remembered that dirty napkin with Gator's phone number on it.

As soon as they got home, Maggie ran up to her room, and pulled it out from under her mattress. She quietly made to the phone and called. The line rang three times before Gator answered the phone.

He said, "Hello."

Maggie blurted out, "I just found out I'm pregnant!"

After a brief moment of silence, Gator asked, "Who is this?"

Feeling stupid, Maggie murmured, "This is Maggie, the red headed girl from Courtney's Halloween party."

Gator asked, "Why are you telling me that you're pregnant?"

At this point Maggie was livid and said, "You're the only guy I've ever been with, so that makes you the father!"

Gator said, "Can't you just get an abortion?"

Maggie felt like this was a dead end, and wanted to avoid any further humiliation.

Maggie said, "Never mind, you're a loser, I'll take care of this myself!"

About the time Maggie hung up the phone, she heard the front door open, and knew it was time. Maggie's anger was quickly replaced with panic. She inched closer to the top of the stairs to listen.

Maggie could hear her mother sobbing.

Her father shouted, "What?"

Then, he yelled at her to come down. Maggie sat down at their table when she got to the kitchen. She kept silent while her mother cried, and her father ranted. Maggie was flooded with a broad range of emotions, but the most dominate one was shame

Too scared to say a word, Maggie sat quietly, and listened to her parent's plan of action. They had already contacted the church. Father Darren was making arrangements for Maggie to be placed in a home for unwed mothers. Maggie would stay there, until she gave birth. The baby would be transferred to an orphanage, and she would return home to resume her life. Her parents informed Maggie that she would be leaving after Thanksgiving. Their family was coming in the holiday, and they didn't want her absence to cause speculation.

Thanksgiving was only a week away. With all the tension in their house, that week couldn't go by fast enough. When their family arrived for Thanksgiving dinner, Maggie's mother gave a final warning of keeping the pregnancy to herself. She watched as her mother greeted everyone and acted as if nothing was out of the ordinary. Maggie wanted to tell Avery, but she knew her mother would not approve. Instead, Maggie did her best to pretend that she was happy. Before long, everyone had gone home and Avery returned to base at Fort Smith. Maggie's parents instructed her to pack a few bags, because she was leaving for St. Anthony's in the morning.

Maggie was very sleepy, and assumed that the medication was beginning to wear off. She wondered how long she'd been awake, but couldn't see the wall clock in her dark room. Just as Maggie closed her eyes, somebody flipped a light switch.

That chipper person said, "Good morning!"

3

MEMORY OF ST. ANTHONY'S

Breakfast that morning consisted of, scrambled eggs, sausage and biscuits with white gravy. That was a step up from the usual tasteless grits they served every morning. Maggie was pleased to see that the new aide had returned. She was skillfully gentle at feeding, and cleaning Maggie up. The new aide was more talkative this morning.

The new aide said, "My name is Julie and I'll be taking care of you during the day."

Maggie thought, "Finally, someone who seems to care about me!"

When Maggie was finished eating, Julie cleaned her up and said, "I'll see you for lunch."

Maggie felt exhausted, and decided to take a nap. Just as she was about to drift off, a man walked into her room. Upon further examination, Maggie realized the man was a priest. She smiled nervously.

She thought, "He must be here to read me my

last rites."

The priest must have noticed the worry on Maggie's face because he said "God hasn't told me about any divine appointments today."

He reassured her that he was just making his rounds for the week. Maggie let out a giggle because she enjoyed his dry humor. He sat next to Maggie in silence which gave her peace. Having a priest in her room created a calm atmosphere, but his presence also triggered memories of her time spent at St. Anthony's.

It was the day after Thanksgiving, and only her mother went with Maggie. Maggie studied her mother as she drove. Her mother was hunched over, while tightly gripping the steering wheel. Her eyes were fixed on the road ahead, and the expression of despair was frozen on her face. Three hours of their trip was mostly quite. However, the tension between them was very loud. No longer able to stand it Maggie broke the ice.

She said, "Mom, I am so sorry. Please don't hate me."

Maggie's mother did not respond, instead she sobbed for at least thirty minutes. The further away they traveled from home, the colder Maggie felt towards her mom. An emotional distance began to emerge. Maggie wanted her mother to comfort her, and reassure her that everything would be okay. Maggie needed to sob, while being held by her mother. Maggie desperately wanted the emotional wound to stop bleeding, but this kind of cut required more than just a band-aid. Maggie felt the need to patch up their relationship, but she knew there was nothing she could say or do at that point to change what had happened. Maggie knew that to recover from an injury this deep, the soul would just need time to heal.

When they reached their destination, Maggie's mother helped carry in her bags. She signed some paperwork, hugged Maggie and left. Maggie stood there for a while in utter disbelief.

Maggie blurted out, "That's it, just sweep me under the rug like I'm some kind of dirty, trashy secret."

Followed by her angry statement was enormous shame, and quickly her cheeks began to burn with embarrassment. An old woman dressed in black garb from head to toe escorted Maggie to her room. Without a single word between the two, they walked down several halls before arriving at Maggie's bedroom. The nun opened the door and waved Maggie in.

With a forced smile the nun said, "I'm Sister Agnus." Then commented, "You might want to get washed up for dinner."

As Sister Agnus closed Maggie's door to her new room, a sense of dread crept in.

Maggie thought, "This is not at all what I anticipated."

In fact, Maggie was sure she would find a warm comfy bed draped with a hand-stitched quilt. At the very least she thought their walls would be adorned with religious paintings, and possibly monks chanting in the background. Perhaps sweet little old ladies, dressed as nuns, would welcome Maggie with open arms. She imagined that the food would be like Grandma style cooking, and was already craving meatloaf.

Instead, what she got was a thin mattress supported by a wooden frame, and a musty old cover. The only wall covering in Maggie's room was the white paint that covered the center blocks, and a crucifix above her bed. Her assigned room had only a bed, and two other pieces of furniture. A wobbly old dresser, and a night stand. On her night stand was a lamp and Bible. Sister Agnus was certainly no sweet little old lady either. Rather, she was cold, distant, and kind of large.

Apparently it was time for dinner because Sister Agnus stuck her head in Maggie's room.

She said, "Lets go before all the food is gobbled up!"

Maggie followed Sister Agnus to the main dining hall. She was instructed to get a tray, and go through the line. After Maggie got her food, which was not meatloaf, she spotted an empty table by a window. What they served for dinner was just depressing! Her first meal was peanut butter slopped between two pieces of stale bread.

After dinner, a few girls went to the day room to play a game of cards. In no mood to socialize, Maggie just went to her room. She felt like a criminal in prison, or a crazy person in a mental institution.

She thought, "This place is not comfy at all!"

Maggie was able to isolate herself for a whole month, but being so lonely began to wear on her. She realized how much she missed her mother and father. Christmas was a few days away, and Maggie really hoped to get a visit. She called home.

Her mother answered the phone and said, "Hello."

Maggie asked, "Are you and dad coming to see me?"

Her mother replied, "I am coming, but your father has to stay home, and tend to things on the farm."

Maggie said, "Okay! I can't wait to see you!"

They said their goodbyes and ended their phone conversation.

Christmas day had arrived, and so had Maggie's mother. She ran into her mother's arms, and sobbed into her neck.

Maggie whispered, "Oh mom, I've missed you so much!"

After a long embrace Maggie showed her mother around, and ended the tour in her room. They sat on her bed, and talked about everything they would do together when Maggie got back home.

Her mother hugged Maggie again. As her mother got up to leave, she paused.

Her mother said, "I almost forgot."

Her mother pulled a present from her bag, and set it on the dresser. She kissed Maggie on the forehead.

Her mom said, "Merry Christmas."

Then she left. Maggie leaned back on her bed, and stared at the gift for a long time. The wrapping paper was striped like a candy cane with a large red bow on top.

Maggie thought, "This is the splash of color I needed!"

Eventually curiosity won, so she gently opened the package. A rather ordinary looking cardboard box was exposed under all that frilly wrapping paper. With her finger nail, Maggie punctured the tape that held its top flaps together. Inside there was a folded note addressed "To Daddy's Little Girl". Under that note was bright red tissue paper, which concealed a hand-stitched lap quilt with a hint of her mother's flare. Also included, were two apples, three oranges, and a pair of her father's wool socks.

Maggie could tell that her mother had put a lot of time and thought into the quilt. The quilt was bursting with color, implying that her mother must have known the surroundings were so bland. What Maggie loved most about her quilt was that there was no specific pattern, or symmetry. A cluster of different shapes and sizes clearly reflected the many characteristics of Maggie's personality. Maggie recognized much of the fabric sewn into her quilt. One piece was from her communion dress, another piece was from her baby blanket, and a few other pieces were from her beloved grandmother's handkerchief.

Maggie felt as though her chest had caved in. A whimper escaped her mouth, and she shook all over. Her breathing became irregular and shallow. She couldn't get enough air in her lungs . Maggie felt faint, and knew she was hyperventilating. She remembered seeing her mother have these spells. Her father would usually bring a paper bag to breath into. Maggie looked around the room, but could find nothing similar to a paper bag. Unable to calm down, it became more difficult for her to breath.

Maggie's ears rang. Her vision was fading to black. All she could see was the quilt, which lay in her trembling hands. Maggie buried her face in the quilt. She was comforted by the smell of her mother and of home. Still clutching her quilt closely, Maggie put on her father's oversized wool socks, and began reading his note.

It said, "Dear Maggie, I have loved you since the day you were born. I'm glad you're doing the right thing for yourself and the baby. We all make mistakes, but that doesn't mean that life can't still go on. Your mother and I are looking forward to the day you come back home. We will help you get through this. We love you, and will see you soon. I sent those socks you love to wear at Christmas time, and yes Santa still makes practice runs! Love Daddy."

Her shoulders dropped and she sank into her bed. Maggie finally acknowledged the sadness that had followed her around since arriving at St. Anthony's. In a moment's notice, the emotions that Maggie worked hard to suppress had now reared its ugly head. That wave of emotion caused Maggie to curl up into a fetal position, and sob hysterically into her quilt. Exhausted, she finally fell asleep.

The next morning her head, and swollen eyes were throbbing. Other than that, Maggie felt somewhat refreshed, like she needed a good cry. Determined to be more social, she learned how to play poker. Poker was appealing to Maggie because the nuns had rules against gambling.

One day she overheard some girls talking about keeping their baby. Up until that point she hadn't even considered that as an option. Maggie never got involved in those conversations. After all, the father of her baby was not even a boyfriend. Rather, he was just a fling who advised her to get an abortion.

Maggie just wanted this baby out of her, so she could get back home, and be normal again. It wasn't until the third month of pregnancy that Maggie felt the baby move. Movement in her belly solidified the reality of a living baby growing inside of her.

Maggie had only been warned about having a bad reputation, the pain of labor, and how stretched out her body would be. However, not one person warned Maggie about the connection in her soul to this baby. No one mentioned that she would fall in love with this baby. Maggie was not warned that she would be heartbroken, when she left the baby there. Maggie had a feeling that this would change her in ways she never imagined.

Prior to feeling the baby move, Maggie had only dwelt on the fear, and anxiety surrounding the pain of birth. Maggie now worried about what would happen to the baby without her. This would prove to be a struggle that Maggie was ill equipt for, and one that would almost cripple her spirit.

Over the next three months she spoke more openly about her feeling with the other girls. Maggie couldn't believe that she was trying to work out a plan to keep the baby.

At seven months pregnant, Maggie decided to ask her parents if they would reconsider their plan of action concerning her baby. Maggie went to the office of St. Anthony's and placed a call home.

Her mother answered, "Hello."

Nervously she exclaimed, "Mom, I can't do it, I can't give up this baby, I want to raise it!"

On the other end of the line, Maggie heard her mother take a deep breath, and sigh.

Her mother said, "Maggie honey, this decision has already been made, you must remember what's best for you and the baby. Besides, the adoptive parents have already been notified with a due date, and they're waiting with anticipation for their new little baby."

Those words stung. Maggie was shocked by her mothers lack of feelings for this baby.

Her mother said, "Well I have a lot to do, so I need to let you go, but try not to think so much about the baby. Love you, bye."

At a loss of words and sort of numb, Maggie hung the phone up. She couldn't control the anger that began to boil inside her. Later that night she went to bed, and embraced her swollen belly. Maggie replayed the conversation with her mother. The answer was no, and there was nothing she could do about it. Maggie despised her mother's disposition, but more than that she hated herself for getting into this predicament in the first place. In order to keep her sanity, Maggie decided to turn off these feelings, and try to ignore the baby's movement. Any time she caught herself entertaining thoughts of the baby, she'd redirect attention to cleaning, or playing cards.

On July 28, 1954, and three days before Maggie's seventeenth birthday was the day she would give birth. She was brought to her knees in the hallway, while on her way to breakfast. A terrible pain shot from her lower back around to her lower abdomen. Clueless, Maggie didn't realize that was only the first contraction.

She screamed, "My baby is going to fall out on the floor."

Sister Agnus restrained a laugh then said, "This is only the beginning of the pain you will feel."

She put Maggie in the wheel chair, and rolled Maggie over to the maternity wing, which was attached to the housing facility of St. Anthony's.

Once Maggie was positioned in the hospital bed Sister Agnus said, "I have to tend to the other girls now, but I'll see you on the other end."

Maggie was in too much pain to say anything but she thought, "Sister Agnus say's the weirdest things!"

The nurse finally came in, but only to inform Maggie that she wasn't the only girl in labor.

Then the nurse said, "we are short staffed, so I can't stay with you the whole time."

Maggie had never experienced so pain in her life. She managed to catch a glimpse of the nurse's name tag, which was Lucy.

Before nurse Lucy left she commented, "be sure to watch the clock, so that you can keep me updated on how far apart your contractions are."

Maggie felt another jarring shot of pain in the bottom half of her body; it was as if she was being ripped from the inside out! She let out an ear piercing scream, and begged nurse Lucy not to leave her alone.

Nurse Lucy said, "don't worry honey, this pain is normal, and every woman feels it, I'll be back in a jiffy to check on you."

Maggie was beyond terrified. She needed her mama and daddy right now! Thirteen hours later her water finally broke, and nurse Lucy told her that she was only half way there.

Maggie wondered if she would die, which explained Sister Agnus' weird comment of seeing her on the other end.

Five hours later, and just enough strength left for one more push, Maggie was successful. She heard the cry of her baby, and thought it was the most beautiful sound she'd ever heard. Then Maggie fell unconscious.

When Maggie awoke, she felt around on her stomach for the baby, but it was gone. She called out for nurse Lucy three times before she came in.

Maggie asked, "Where's my baby?"

Nurse Lucy replied, "The baby is a girl, weighing seven pounds four ounces and doing fine."

Maggie asked, "When can I hold my baby?"

But nurse Lucy said, "That's not possible."

Three days later Sister Agnus showed up.

Sister Agnus said, "Get dressed. Your mother will be here in an hour to collect you."

Maggie got dressed, and sat in the wheel chair.

On the way out Maggie asked, "Could I at least see the baby?"

Nurse Lucy replied, "It would only make it harder, besides the baby has already been transferred to the orphanage."

Maggie was wheeled to her room, where she found her things already packed up. Sitting next to her things, on the bed, was a stack of papers.

Sister Agnus explained, "We need your signature, so that you can be released, and I need a temporary baby name for the paperwork." She went on to say, "Providing a name is only a technicality, because the adoptive parents almost always change the name."

A technicality or not, Maggie was unprepared to name her baby.

Maggie said, "Name her Mary, after the mother of Jesus."

Maggie pulled out the quilt her mother had made for Christmas.

She asked, "Can you make sure this quilt goes with Mary to her new home?"

Sister Agnus hesitated, but then said, "Only if

you don't cause any trouble when your mother comes to get you."

With tears streaming down her face, Maggie gave Sister Agnus a big hug, and thanked her. They walked out of St. Anthony's together, and met her mother at the car. Maggie got in without even making eye contact with her mother.

Her mother drove away from St. Anthony's, and past the orphanage wing. Maggie wanted to bring her baby home, but fought the urge.

She remembered what Sister Agnus said, "Only if you don't cause any trouble when you leave!"

Maggie wanted to make sure the quilt went home with Mary. That was the only way Mary could have a piece of Maggie, so she kept quiet. Maggie clinched her lips together to keep her sobs silent, but it was impossible to stop the tears from coming. Looking out the window seemed to work because her mother didn't say anything. Her mother must have known that if Maggie spoke, she would lose her composure. Maggie tried hard to shake the empty feeling inside of her, but the overpowering emotion refused to leave. There was no way she could ever forget about the life she carried for nine months. Maggie hoped that Mary would forgive her for this abandonment, but only time would tell.

The day Maggie was released from St. Anthony's Home for Unwed Mothers was her birthday. This fact just brought more sorrow, as she realized this would be a yearly reminder of her baby. Her mother had baked a cake and presented a gift, so

Maggie tried, extra hard, to smile. Her parents, though, could see a certain amount of sorrow in her eyes. They reassured her that by the time school started it would be easier, and surely by graduation this would only be a fuzzy memory. Maggie really wanted her parents to be right, but in her gut she knew the loss she felt would never go away. Maggie accepted that she would just have to get better at faking happiness.

That night Maggie cried herself to sleep. Maggie had planned to stay in bed forever like her mother used to do, but the next day her father came in the room to talk.

He said, "Yesterday was your birthday, and I'm sure it was hard to be in a great mood due to all that's happened lately. The longer you stay in this bed the harder it is to get out. Besides, I need your help mending fences today."

As expected, August rolled around without fail, and school started. Maggie noticed that Priscilla was missing. Later she found out that Priscilla had gotten married over the summer, and wasn't coming back to school. Not having Priscilla there was upsetting, but Maggie's mother thought she was a bad influence anyway. Some of Maggie's classmates asked where she'd gone that previous year. She told them a story her mother provided, which was taking care of her sick grandmother.

Luckily her senior year flew by, and graduation was right around the corner. Maggie couldn't wait to get the heck out of Dodge; the only hold up was her lack of money. That summer she got a job working the concession stand at The Hillbilly Hoe Down in Eureka Springs.

Once again, Maggie's attention was involuntarily yanked from reliving the past when the priest stood up.

He said, "Well I'll be on my way, so you can get some rest."

And out the door he went. Maggie must have nodded off without realizing it because she was awakened by a loud crash. The priest was gone, and her new roommate was not happy about moving in.

4

CRAZY ROOMMATE

To say that Maggie's new room mate was not happy would be an understatement. She was enraged, and in a full-blown temper tantrum kicking, screaming and cursing!

Maggie sarcastically thought, "Oh fun, another loud one, exactly what I needed!"

Nurse Julie walked in with lunch, and was able to talk the crazy lady into cooperation. Maggie thought that was miraculous! After Julie got the crazy lady calm, she fed Maggie her pasta salad surprise, and presented them both with a snack of buttery popcorn. Maggie loved the taste of popcorn. The yummy snack also reminded her of working the concession stand at the Hillbilly Hoe Down. The concession stand was where she met her husband John.

It was a sweltering night in mid July, and the house was packed. Random chatter from the crowd spoke of excitement concerning the show. An occasional customer would yell out their order of popcorn with extra butter, and a coke. It was the tall, handsome cowboy in the corner that caught Maggie's attention.

He was peering at her from under the brim of his big Stetson hat. Maggie was so captivated by his gaze that it took her breath away. Very quickly, Maggie realized that she could get lost in those dark brown eyes. Maggie knew she had to nab the handsome cowboy, who was able to pierce her soul with just a look.

Fortunately, he too felt their connection because without breaking his gaze on Maggie, the cowboy pushed through the mass of people crowding the concession stand.

The cowboy said, "Howdy Ma'am, I'd like to buy a Dr. Pepper."

Maggie responded, "Will that be all?"

He replied, "No. I also want to know what time you get off."

Maggie was speechless as she surveyed the package of manly beauty before her eyes, ripe for the picking. Maggie finally managed to pull herself back together, and answered.

She said, "I get off at Nine."

The cowboy flashed her a smile, tipped his hat and said, "Well gorgeous, I'll see you then!"

Maggie watched him disappear into the crowd.

She thought, "What could he possibly see in me?"

Before long, the show was over, and quitting time had arrived.

The first one out was her cowboy.

He said, "My name is John, and I'd like to walk you to your car."

She agreed and they walked to her car. Maggie and John were so engrossed in their conversation that they continued to stand in the parking lot. They talked for an hour getting to know each other. John told Maggie that he was in town for a rodeo.

John said, "I've been riding horses, and bucking broncos for most of my life, but just recently started competing."

He also said, "I plan to stay in town the rest of that week, and want you to show me around."

Maggie said, "Sure!"

They parted ways, but agreed to meet again that following day in Springdale for the Annual Rodeo of the Ozarks. After spending every day together that week, it was time for Johns return home to Texas.

Maggie asked, "Will I ever hear from you again?"

John answered, "I will write you every day, and call every week if you'll let me!"

She smiled and gave him a long passionate kiss goodbye. Staying true to his word John wrote, and called her often. With each passing day, however, Maggie's desire to be at John's side grew. John's feelings were mutual, he'd felt that something had changed since first laying eyes on his red headed beauty. John had to have Maggie as his bride. Maggie's parents noticed a difference in her as well.

Her father commented, "I haven't seen you this happy since your sixteenth birthday."

It was as if she had come back to life, and her father was thrilled. Maggie and John had a whirl wind romance of six months, and a long distance relationship was no longer sufficient.

In John's last letter he said, "I'm coming back to Arkansas to ask your father for your hand in marriage."

A few days later Maggie returned from work to find John sitting at her kitchen table talking with her parents. He looked even better than she remembered. She ran into his arms, and they embraced.

John whispered, "He said yes."

Maggie looked at her father and mother with surprise. Her mother and father were smiling like they approved.

John then knelt down on one knee.

He asked, "Will you marry me?"

With tears of joy Maggie nodded yes, and John slid an engagement ring on her finger.

Maggie's mother spoke up and said, "Well since John is Protestant, we can arrange the wedding ceremony at The Methodist Church."

Remarkably in only four weeks Maggie's mother was able to make her wedding dress, invite the whole community, and decorate for their reception. Maggie hadn't seen this side of her mother since she was a little girl, and it felt good. Finally the day of Maggie and John's wedding had arrived.

The ceremony was scheduled for one thirty that afternoon at St. Matthew's Methodist Church. The quaint little chapel was located in Berryville, Arkansas. Their wedding day was made more perfect by an inch thick layer of snow, as if God were blessing their union. As Maggie and her father stood in the foyer, she could hear the traditional wedding march being played, which was the signal to start down the isle.

Her father smiled at Maggie and said, "I'm so proud of you!"

Maggie made her way down to the altar where John was standing. She noticed that every pew was full. To settle her nerves, Maggie locked eyes with her eager groom. When they made it to the altar, Maggie's father handed her over to John. Standing at John's side, everyone else seemed to disappear. It was as if Maggie and John were the only people in that place. They exchanged vows, rings, and a kiss to seal the deal. Mr. and Mrs. John Anderson then left the church, and Arkansas to start their new life together in Texas.

John already owned property in Alpine, Texas with more than fifty heads of cattle. They lived in his bunkhouse for two years, while John completed the big house he built for Maggie. After living in the big house for a full year Maggie finally got pregnant, and gave birth to their first son. John named him Thomas after his grandfather, but they ended up calling him

Tom for short.

When Tom was two years old, Maggie's brother Avery received an honorable discharge from the military. Avery got married to his high school sweet heart, bought a house in Berryville, Arkansas, and had a daughter. Avery insisted they name her Ann, after Maggie's middle name. Maggie and John hoped for another child, but after four years of trying they'd already accepted that Tom may be their only child.

Then out of the blue Maggie found out she was pregnant. Maggie's second pregnancy was blighted with so many complications that the doctor prepared her for a miscarriage. The doctor also warned that the prospects of another pregnancy were dim. Maggie was anguished, but John assured her that God was in control.

John said, "If God planted this seed, then God he would bring it to completion."

John's faith was what carried them through. Maggie gave birth to a baby boy and named him Charlie. He was one month early, but still healthy. Maggie was so satisfied in life. She and John were still madly in love; she adored her boys. John had built her a beautiful two-story log cabin, and they were doing well financially. Maggie never realized this level of happiness was possible.

As Tom got older, Maggie could see character traits surfacing that were geared toward the rodeo, and other thrill seeking adventures. Charlie, on the other hand, was more relaxed. He enjoyed participating in local church events. Maggie thought it was funny how brothers with the same parents could be so different. She loved everything about her boys, including their differences.

Tom was naturally gifted at playing football, and after graduation he won a full scholarship to a college in Dallas, Texas. Charlie was sad when Tom moved out, but he was invited to attend summer camp with the Methodist youth group. When Charlie got back from camp, he talked his parents into attending the Methodist church on a more regular basis.

Maggie was happy that Charlie's camp counselor made such an impression on her son. Maggie found out that Charlie's counselor was the Methodist preacher, and was thrilled to become more active. Like Tom promised, he came home for Christmas. Charlie was so excited to see his big brother. Later that day Tom promised to take Charlie for a ride in his new truck. Charlie begged his dad to go with them.

But John said, "Charlie, I'm really busy. You and Tom go have a good time."

However, John would later regret ever letting them leave.

Maggie was distracted by nurse Julie taking her tray, and walking out. The crazy lady jumped up out of her bed. Maggie could hear the crazy lady murmuring under her breath, but couldn't make out what she was saying. She helplessly watched as the crazy lady rummaged through her stuff accusing Maggie of stealing a sweater.

Eventually some staff heard all the commotion, and busted in to intervene. They had to give the crazy lady something to calm her down. Maggie wanted to take a cat nap, but she was too scared to close her eyes, so she just counted the ceiling tiles instead.

In the distance Maggie could hear dinner carts rolling toward her room. Meal time was one of the most enjoyable events for her. Now confined to her bed, Maggie was only able to soar like an eagle with her mind. Luckily Maggie's imagination was fueled by her sense of sight, sound, and smell. Maggie imagined that those food carts were off to the races.

She listened with anticipation for the head cafeteria lady to say, "Okay girls, it's all yours!"

Next would be a flurry of ladies to grab their carts and go.

Maggie thought, "I wonder who will deposit all their trays first, and be quickest to finish."

She was a sucker for the underdog, and wanted the cart, with the bum wheel, to win today. Maggie must have lost track of time, and the food cart derby. It seemed that in no time the cart, with the bum wheel, was in her room. The crazy lady had already been given her tray, and had company to boot! It looked like that lady's sweet son, and some other woman were going to join her for super.

Maggie felt pitiful as she thought, "Look at me, I have to be hand-fed by random nurses because I can't feed myself."

She thought, "Just great! This might be even

more degrading with an audience!"

Just as Julie put the first bite of food in Maggie's mouth, the crazy lady stood up on her bed. In a fit of rage, she threw her pudding cup at the visiting woman's head. Maggie's watched as her crazy roommate pointed a boney finger in her son's face.

The crazy lady shouted, "I don't know who you are, or why you're spying on me, but if you don't get that hooker out of my room, I'm gonna scratch out her eyeballs!"

Maggie's room was completely silent because everybody's jaw was on the floor. In all the confusion nurse Julie jumped up to intervene, and accidently left a spoonful of English peas in Maggie's mouth.

The crazy lady's son said, "Mama, it's Danny and this is my wife, Ann, remember?"

Julie heard Maggie gagging on peas, and yelled, "Code blue, I need some help!"

Another nurse rushed in, and flung Maggie on her side. A few more nurses ran in to help; they managed to sit Maggie up, and preformed the Heimlich maneuver on her. After a couple of squeezes Maggie spewed green peas all over the crazy lady.

Full-blown chaos had erupted. Covered in regurgitated English peas, Maggie's crazy roommate ran out of their room.

The crazy lady screamed, "Help! Help! This old lady has a demon, and she's trying to get me!"

Maggie thought, "Woman, you'd better be glad I can't walk, because I might hurt you!"

Maggie's anger made it impossible to sleep. After her new roommate completely freaked out, they put her to sleep with a shot. Maggie was stuck with her anger, and the crazy lady's snoring. Finally her anger subsided, and Maggie was able to relax. Just as Maggie closed her eyes, however, she felt a tapping on her forehead. Maggie's eyelids flapped up like scrolls to see, none other than, the crazy lady about five inches away. All Maggie could think about was the outburst she witnessed earlier.

Maggie recalled the crazy roommate telling her son that if he didn't get that hooker out of her room she was going scratch her eyeballs out!

Maggie thought, "Clearly the crazy lady was talking about her daughter-in-law, but could she have gotten mixed up?"

Naturally Maggie was terrified especially when the crazy lady leaned even closer.

She whispered, "I'm breaking out of here, and you're coming with me!"

The crazy lady pushed the wheel chair next to Maggie's bed, and slid her into it. Feeling helpless, Maggie simply had to watch this scene play out, and pray she didn't fall.

Maggie's expression of terror must have been evident, because the crazy lady smiled.

Then she said, "Don't mess in your britches just yet; I'll have you back in time to enjoy your crappy breakfast."

The crazy lady put on a doctor's coat, which she had snatched after that creative diversion earlier.

She whispered, "In order to pull this off I need a patient, and you're just in the wrong place at the wrong time."

Maggie didn't think her life could get much worse, until her pinky toe got tangled in the blanket on their way out. Just before Maggie passed out from the pain, the crazy lady wrestled her free. Maggie panicked as they crept out of their room, and into the hallway. Halfway down the hall, her pinky toe was still throbbing, but at least terror had past. Maggie's panic was replaced with a sense of adventure.

One of the nurses had gone out for a smoke break, and left the back door propped open with a brick. Much to their surprise, an urgent call distracted that smoker nurse. Their exit door was left unguarded. The crazy lady wheeled Maggie out, and noticed an unfinished cigarette still on the window seal. She grabbed it, and took a long drag. The crazy lady went into a coughing fit, and blew their cover.

The owner of that cigarette flew through the back door said, "Ladies, you had better get your butts back in that bed, before anybody else finds out what's going on."

Then she turned to the crazy lady and said, "Promise me that you won't kidnap Maggie again, and I'll come get you for a smoke break next time."

The crazy lady agreed as she stomped back in. The smoker nurse forgot Maggie outside, but before closing the door was reminded by the crazy lady.

The crazy lady asked, "Hey! Where's my partner in crime?"

The smoker nurse turned around, and went back outside to grab the handles of Maggie's wheelchair.

Maggie was rolled over the threshold of hopelessness, and back into that bottomless pit of Hell. Right before Maggie was sucked back into Grandview Nursing Home, something caught her attention. By the light of a full moon, she could see majestic mountains! Maggie sensed that she wasn't in Texas anymore!

The smoker nurse got Maggie and her roommate tucked into bed. She could hear the crazy lady snickering like a little school girl.

Maggie thought, "If I wasn't so puzzled about the scenery change outside, I might be amused as well."

She wondered, "How long have I been back in Arkansas?"

Totally pooped, Maggie just wanted to get some shut eye, but she couldn't stop thinking about the accident that killed her son.

5

HEAVENLY DREAM

Four days before Christmas Tom had come home from college to stay for the holidays. Charlie wanted to ride in Tom's new truck, so he hounded his big brother.

Finally, Tom said, "All right already, lets go!"

Maggie warned them to be careful because the roads might be iced over. Tom reassured her that he'd be extra cautious as he kissed her forehead. A couple of hours passed, and the boys were not home yet. Maggie had a feeling that something terrible had happened. She called Terry, a member of their church and the chief of police, to ask if he could check it out. The search for Tom and Charlie began immediately. Two hours later, Maggie heard a knock at their door. She and John ran to answer it. Standing in their doorway was two police officers. They asked to come in, and suddenly Maggie couldn't breathe.

John asked, "Have you found my boys?

Officer Terry said, “Yes. We need you to come to the morgue, and identify one of the boys.”

The second officer said, “The other boy is in critical condition at Memorial Hospital.”

The police escorted Maggie and John to the morgue. The mortician pulled back a white sheet to reveal Charlie’s face. Maggie let out an awful cry, and ran over to hold her dead son. John finally came to Maggie’s side, but he couldn’t bear to look at Charlie.

John grabbed her and said, “We have to go check on Tom now!”

Maggie felt torn. She needed to go check on her oldest son, but that meant leaving Charlie. John had to pull her off of Charlie, and forcefully put her in their car. Once they got to Memorial Hospital, Maggie had switched gears, and was ready to put her energy into Tom. John found the doctor taking care of Tom.

John asked, “Is my son, Tom Anderson, okay?”

The doctor answered, “Tom has suffered a major head injury, and is in a coma.”

The doctor said, “I was told that your son flat-lined moments after the paramedic’s arrived on the scene. He died due to significant blood lose. Luckily they were able to resuscitate him.”

He stated, “If the swelling in his brain does not go down, then we’ll have to relieve pressure with surgery.”

Maggie asked, "Is my son going to die?"

The doctor answered, "Mrs. Anderson we are doing everything possible to prevent death, but to be honest we're not sure he can survive something like this."

Officer Terry sat in the waiting room with Maggie and John.

Terry said, "I arrived on the scene, and saw Tom first. He was lying on the pavement next to what used to be the guard rail. Apparently he was thrown from the truck upon impact with a deer."

Terry paused to wipe the tears from his eyes and collect himself.

He continued, "Charlie's body wasn't found until they were able to safely get down to the river below."

John wept loudly while Maggie held him. She was still in shock, and felt rather numb.

Officer Terry explained, "The roads were slick, and there are a lot of deer in that area. I based my theory on the tire marks and shattered glass. I concluded that Tom was thrown through the windshield before the truck ran off the bridge and into the river."

He went on to say, "The whole cab of the truck was submerged. Charlie was unable to get loose from his seat belt and drowned."

Maggie felt sick. She always stressed the importance of wearing their seat belt, but that was what kept Charlie underwater. Maggie felt responsible for his death.

Charlie's funeral was three days later on Christmas eve, and Tom was still in a coma. It seemed like Maggie was outside of her body watching a movie. Seeing her dead son in a casket, just seemed so surreal. Maggie had cried so much in the days leading up to Charlie's funeral that she was empty, and void of all emotion at his actual service. Maggie was numb while she stared down at Charlie in his Sunday suit. Her broken heart hurt so badly that she could not even find the words to express her pain. The hope of Tom's recovery was the only thing that kept Maggie from ending her own life.

A week after the accident Tom woke up, and saw his parents sitting at his bed side. John called a nurse to let them know he was awake. After checking his vitals the nurse told them she'd go get the doctor.

Tom looked at his mother, and started crying.

He said, "I'm sorry Mama, please forgive me."

Maggie grabbed his hand and said, "Its okay baby I'm here, and you're gonna be okay."

The doctor had warned them not to tell Tom about Charlie, until he was more stable.

But Tom said, "Mama, I know about Charlie, I saw him with Jesus!"

Maggie kept quiet, but wondered how Tom knew that Charlie had died.

Recalling such a tragic event brought back a

sadness that Maggie had already dealt with. Confined to a bed in the nursing home was not a good place to get depressed, so she just went to sleep.

In her dream Maggie was standing in a massive entryway. The place looked like Grand Central Station, but far more exquisite. The structure's interior was finished in gleaming white marble, but brighter than any white Maggie had ever seen before. Without any fear, or hesitation Maggie ventured further into this magnificent building.

Along the western wall of this enormous building was a string of waiting rooms that looked similar to those in a hospital. Each room was divided from the other by a clear glass wall. Separating the waiting rooms from the main lobby was also a glass wall. Every waiting room was empty except one, and Maggie recognized the girl in that room.

That girl had short blonde hair with bangs, and beautiful bright blue eyes. Her name was Priscilla, and she was Maggie's best friend from high school. Maggie entered in, and walked over to Priscilla.

Maggie asked, "Why are you here?"

With a blank face, Priscilla answered, "This is the waiting room for Hell, and that's where I'm going."

Maggie was very disturbed by Priscilla's expression because she looked as though any hope of ever leaving that place had been lost. Maggie wanted to help Priscilla, but something compelled her to keep moving. Maggie exited Hell's waiting room.

She became aware of a stream that ran from the northern wall to the southern wall of this huge lobby, dividing it right down the middle. Instinctively Maggie knew that she was supposed to swim across. As she stepped in, her body sank straight to the bottom. Immediately Maggie bobbed back up like a cork, and realized that instead of water she was swimming in some mysterious foggy substance. She reached the other side, and climbed out. Maggie wasn't even wet.

Intrigued, Maggie watched a court house materialized right before her eyes on the eastern wall. A bright light seemed to be coming from inside the courthouse. Several massive columns supported the overhang in front. A tall set of stairs trickled down seamlessly to personally invite Maggie to climb them.

Suddenly it appeared as if a director on set called, "Action," because a rush of human traffic raced up and down the steps.

What seemed like business as usual for those people running around was a surprise to Maggie.

She wondered, "Why are they in such a hurry? Do they not realize the beauty of this place?"

Before Maggie had a chance to think another thought, all that action simply ceased like the same unseen director yelled, "Cut!"

All those people, just a moment before, were running around, yet now were frozen in time and space. Maggie could see an angel coming out of the courthouse and floating down the stairs. The angel was heading toward Maggie. Maggie soon realized that, like those people, she too had become frozen.

God's Angel had dark wavy hair, and huge white feathered wings. The angel's robe was white. A gold cord was tied around his waist, and kris-crossed over his chest. God's Angel was surrounded by a bright light, which began to flicker as he got closer to Maggie.

They were not able to move again, until the angel passed them by. Maggie continued up the steps, but stopped before reaching the top. She saw a young boy trip, and fall over an untied shoe lace. She ran over, and swooped the boy up to set him back on his feet.

Maggie noticed that right inside the courthouse sat twelve men at a table, and Jesus standing at its end. Jesus motioned, with his hand, for Maggie and the boy to sit in two vacant chairs. As they sat down, open Bibles appeared on the table in front of them. From behind Maggie, Jesus pointed to a portion of scripture in her Bible. Maggie's eyes focused on where his finger pointed, but just as she was about to read that scripture, she woke up!

Coming back to reality was never all that fun, but this was awful! Maggie agonized over what that scripture could have said. She even tried going back to sleep, but that didn't work. Instead, she went over every detail with a fine tooth comb, and hoped to find a clue to this dream's meaning.

Maggie thought, "I haven't thought about Priscilla in years."

She wondered, "What was that place? Who was that little boy?"

While mulling over the dream, it seemed vaguely familiar to her, but she couldn't figure out why. Then it came to her! Maggie remembered, the first time she had this dream was during her stay at St. Anthony's Home for Unwed Mothers. The dream occurred while she was pregnant with her baby girl! Maggie recalled feeling the same way then too. She woke up confused; tried to go back to sleep, but couldn't. She recalled grabbing the bible from her night stand, and frantically flipping through it pages, but found nothing. Maggie remembered falling to her knees at eight months pregnant in frustration.

She remembered praying, "God, please let me have that dream again, or reveal its meaning me!"

In the sixty years since that dream, Maggie had petitioned God numerous times with her request. She was left to wonder if her prayers were falling on deaf ears.

Maggie thought, "Well why would God wait sixty years to answer my prayer of having this dream again?"

"And what about its meaning, is that still another sixty years down the road?" Maggie thought sarcastically.

Maggie heard what sounded like gas coming from the crazy lady's bed, and her anger began to boil rapidly. The smell was far worse than the sound. Maggie thought she'd pass out, but the air conditioner kicked on to help circulate the overpowering smell of human feces.

The rest of that night was dreadful. By morning nurse Julie walked in with breakfast, and gagged.

Julie said, "Pew wee it smells like a dirty diaper in here!"

The crazy lady smiled, and replied, "You shouldn't have given me so much popcorn!"

Julie commented, "Don't worry Priscilla, I won't make that mistake again. I just hope you didn't kill Maggie with that poison!"

Maggie thought, "You have no idea how I suffered!"

While feeding Maggie, Julie would occasionally say something to the crazy lady. Maggie was confused, though, because Julie was calling the crazy lady by the name of Priscilla. Maggie wondered if this crazy lady in her room was, in fact, Priscilla from her past! That might explain part of her dream the night before.

Julie left, and Priscilla started crying. Maggie had already noticed that this crazy lady, now known as Priscilla, wasn't as chipper as she was yesterday. The nursing staff must have picked up on her mood too because the smoker nurse had been in to see if she wanted to take a smoke break.

But Priscilla responded, “Go away I’m tired!”

Even though Priscilla had done nothing but make Maggie mad, she still felt bad for her, and wanted to help.

She thought, “How could I help her if I can’t even help myself.”

Then it dawned on her! She could pray for Priscilla!

Maggie prayed, “Dear God, please give Priscilla peace for whatever’s bothering her, and just bless her, in Jesus’ name, Amen.”

And just like that, the priest walked in.

Maggie thought, “Wow that was a quick answer to prayer!”

The priest commented, “You look more intrigued today.”

Maggie’s eyes lit up, and she smiled at him.

She thought, “Ding, ding, ding, we have a winner!”

So he sat in a chair next to Maggie. Maggie noticed that the priest had his Bible today. Before she could blink, he grabbed her hand.

He said, “Every once in a while, God speaks to me in a very clear voice, but most of the time he just speaks to me through scripture.”

He paused for a moment to gather himself.

He said, “Last night while I was praying for you, God told me to read scripture to you every day.”

Priscilla must have been listening in because she said, “Can you read to me too?”

The priest looked back at Maggie. She gave him a quick smile.

He replied, “The more, the merrier.”

Oddly, the funk that hovered over Priscilla most of that morning had vanished. The priest only got through the first two chapters of Matthew in the new testament when lunch arrived. He patted Maggie on the arm, and told them that he’d be back later to read more.

After the priest left, Priscilla commented, “Grandma Harrison would tell that story of Christ every Christmas while on the way to Mass.”

Now Maggie knew for sure that her new room mate, the crazy lady, was indeed the same Priscilla from her past!

Julie presented lunch with a frown asking, “Yummy, Road-Kill-Soup anyone?”

Even Julie knew the chicken and rice was nasty. Maggie laughed out loud, and surprised everyone in the room. Sound had not escaped Maggie’s mouth in years.

Julie found Maggie’s laugh to be contagious and she said, “At least the cornbread has a sweet flavor, and your tangy fruit punch will help wash it down!”

Laughing at her own wit, Julie was now hunched over, and fighting for air between giggles. Priscilla wasn't sure what was going on.

She asked, "Was this food really killed on the road?"

Julie straightened up, and with a pleasant face said, "No, Ms. Priscilla, I was only kidding."

Then she collected their finished trays and said, "Good day ladies."

Maggie really liked Julie a lot, and wanted to find out more about her, but wasn't sure how that would work. Maggie smiled when she thought about how Julie made her laugh.

Maggie was in a good mood until Priscilla said, "I wonder why that priest would tell us a Christmas story when the next holiday is Halloween."

Hearing Priscilla reference Christmas again triggered a flashback of Maggie's worst Christmas ever. After Charlie's funeral, Maggie went back to Memorial Hospital, and stayed at Tom's side. She already lost one son, and was determined not to lose the other. Maggie prayed fervently for Tom to live and be healed.

Mean while, back at home John took down all the Christmas decorations. He put away the unopened Christmas gifts involving Charlie before Tom returned home. Besides, John had certainly lost any Christmas spirit. At the sight of anything festive, John became infuriated. Maggie's prayer to keep Tom alive was answered, and after spending only two weeks in the hospital he was released. However, the road to recovery was not easy. Tom lost his football scholarship, and progress with physical therapy was slow.

Eventually he regained most of his strength, but was informed that his football career was over. Maggie's parents offered Tom a job on their farm. They told Tom that he could stay in the bunk house as long as he needed to. So, Tom moved to Arkansas, and quickly discovered that he had a real talent for farming. He also spent a lot of time with his Uncle Avery, who helped Tom grieve Charlie's death.

John stayed in the anger stage of grief for a very long time. Maggie put her feelings on the back burner, in order to help her husband. In time, John opened up to their pastor about his anger with himself. Working with their pastor, really helped John through the ongoing process of grief. He even admitted to Maggie that, for a while, he was mad at God for not saving Charlie. Later, however, John realized that it was just Charlie's time to go.

Of course, Maggie still had her bad days, but was thankful for the fourteen years that she got to spend with Charlie. John told her that it seemed like he'd lost both sons because Tom moved to Arkansas. They decided to start making more trips to visit. Maggie was excited to see her family, and those glorious Arkansas mountains!

6

CHURCH GRANDMA

Maggie studied Priscilla's wrinkled face.

She wondered, "Gosh, I hope my face looks better than that!"

She had so much to tell her old friend, but her voice box just refused to work.

Priscilla acknowledged Maggie's stare and said, "My son Danny tells me that he married your niece Ann." Priscilla went on to say, "And if you're planning to kill me tonight for calling her a hooker, just know I sleep with one eye open!"

Maggie just rolled her eyes.

She thought, "Priscilla has clearly lost it."

Maggie searched her memory bank to find her niece Ann, but the last memory she had was about two years after Charlie's death. She and John had taken a road trip from Texas to Arkansas for Ann's wedding.

Maggie thought, "If Priscilla is telling the truth, then I am now related to my crazy old friend by marriage."

Maggie continued probing her mind, until she found what she was looking for. And there it was, she remembered seeing Avery walk Ann down the isle. Maggie also remembered that Priscilla, the mother of the groom, had arrived late and smelled of alcohol.

Priscilla's late arrival was such an embarrassing distraction for Danny. When it came time for the priest to ask if anyone disagreed with the union of Ann and Danny, Priscilla stood up.

Maggie rushed over to quiet her, but was unsuccessful.

Priscilla shouted, "Look here little Misses' perfect, I bet they don't know about Gator!"

Maggie's immediate reaction was to cover the mouth that threatened expose her secret! What happened instead was more of a slap in Priscilla's face. They were both escorted out of the sanctuary by ushers. Priscilla left, and Maggie apologized to Ann and her new husband Danny. Embarrassed, John and Maggie left as soon as they said goodbye to Tom.

On the way home John asked, "Who is Gator?"

Maggie figured now was the time to tell John everything. Maggie was afraid that John would think she was a horrible person for getting into that situation. It was hard to tell John about the fling with

Gator and his total rejection of her. Maggie found it far more difficult, however, to tell John about the baby she had given up. Although, the more Maggie opened up, the softer John's expression got. John looked at Maggie with complete compassion.

He said, "Honey, I'm sorry you experienced such a jerk early on, and I'm sorry you had to go through the loss of that baby alone, but why did you not tell me until now?"

Maggie replied, "I was afraid you wouldn't marry me if you knew, or that you would leave me because I didn't tell you sooner."

John had already pulled off the road into a rest stop. He got out, and went around to Maggie's side. She opened the car door.

John said, "I need a hug!"

Maggie giggled, got out, and kissed John.

Then Maggie said, "I am so in love with you!"

They got back in their car, and went home. That same year John started feeling tired all the time, so Maggie took him in for some tests. At age fifty, he was diagnosed with testicular cancer. Maggie and John agreed not to worry their family. After all, Tom was doing so well in Arkansas.

Six months later after surgery, and lots of radiation treatment John was in remission. They were relieved when John received a clean bill of health, but still had a feeling that this wasn't the last they'd see of cancer. The earth didn't stop spinning for cancer, so life went on. John remained in the cattle business, until one day he noticed a few of his cows trudging through, what look and smelled like, petroleum.

After making some inquires around town, John contacted a local oil company to start the process of leasing his property for minerals. Soon after signing that mineral lease, John sold every head of his cattle. The oil company got a permit, prepared the site and rigged up. It took a good while before they struck enough oil to pay any royalties, and Maggie was beginning to worry that they sold their cattle off too soon. Everything worked out, and they rarely went without. Now they had more time to spend together.

Apparently God knew Maggie needed to spend more time with John, and that raising cattle would not be possible in the near future. Seven years later John was admitted for tests, and the results were clear. John's cancer was back with a vengeance, but this time in his lungs. The malignant tumor was in a portion of his lungs that could not be removed, so radiation was the only treatment available. Maggie was unprepared for the year that followed. She had to watch her strong husband wither away to nothing. Every day John would get a little more weaker. Maggie feared that she couldn't survive without him.

Maggie felt so selfish at times because she knew that he wanted to die, but she wasn't ready to let him go. A full year of chemotherapy proved unsuccessful, and John's immune system was annihilated. Maggie could see John's torment, and could not handle seeing him suffer any longer to hold on. They decided it was time to inform the family that John was dying. Tom came down from Arkansas, and told Maggie that he'd stay in Texas as long as she needed him to. Maggie tried to be strong, but it was getting more difficult.

She often thought, "Who is going to be strong for me when John dies?"

Surrounded by his family, John made a last request that took Maggie by surprise.

John said, "I want us to open the Christmas gifts I put away after Charlie died."

Tom climbed up in the attic, and brought them down. Charlie had bought them all a gift. John opened his gift first, and found a black felt cowboy hat.

Tom hesitated, not sure if he could handle the emotion.

With a smile, John said, "Tom, I don't have all day!"

Tom pulled back the wrapping paper to see Charlie's old bible! Maggie opened her gift and found a beautiful necklace with a crucifix pendant. Tom helped her put it on.

In tears, John said, "Charlie was so proud that he found that necklace, and knew you would love it."

Tom couldn't hold himself together any longer, and left the room.

John looked at Maggie with peace in his eyes.

He said, “It’s time.”

Maggie kissed his lips.

She replied, “Be sure to give Charlie a kiss for me.”

Then Maggie laid her head on his chest.

She whispered, “I’ll be okay John, you just go make sure they’re not cutting any corners on my mansion.”

Maggie laid there on John’s chest, until his heart quit beating, and he breathed his last breath. Tom came back in the room and held his mother, until the ambulance arrived to take his father’s body to the funeral home. Maggie and Tom did their best to clean John’s sick room, but they needed a break; the stench of death would have to wait until morning.

Maggie woke early the next morning, and found Tom busy cleaning the room where John died. He was on his hands and knees scrubbing the floor with bleach water. At first he didn’t notice her presence in the room.

Maggie said. “You should have woke me up, so I could help.”

When Tom looked up at his mother, she could tell he’d been up all night crying.

He said, “Let me finish this, it’s comforting to know I’m helping you.”

Before Tom could say another word, Maggie had already grabbed a rag.

She said, “Well then, let’s tackle this

together."

They stayed in John's old sick room for three solid hours cleaning, reminiscing, and crying together.

Maggie looked at Tom and said, "You never finished telling me about when you saw Charlie with Jesus."

Tom replied, "I wasn't sure you wanted to hear the rest of it."

A tear rolled down Maggie's cheek.

She said, "I'm ready now."

Tom explained, "When I hit the deer I could feel my body being hurled forward through glass and ripping my skin. The wind was knocked out of me when I landed on the pavement. Right before going unconscious, I heard a big splash, then I blacked out. Next, it felt like I was being pulled away from my body, and when my eyes opened I was looking down on the paramedics performing CPR. Officer Terry was bent over my body, and praying. Then, everything went black except one beam of light coming from above. The darkness vanished as I got closer to the light, and that's when I realized what was going on."

Tom went on, "Next, I could see Jesus wearing a crown that looked like a rainbow. Charlie was standing next to him. Charlie told me that I had to go back because it wasn't my time yet. Charlie hugged me, and told me I was supposed to take care of you."

Maggie hugged Tom and said, "Thanks Tom,

for telling me."

In some strange way, hearing Tom's experience comforted Maggie! John's funeral service was three days later. John had prearranged to be cremated. He told Maggie that after losing their son, the picture of Charlie in a casket was burned into his mind, and he didn't want Maggie to have that mental image of her husband as well.

Maggie reassured Tom that she'd be okay. After all, John had maintained a life insurance policy over the years, that would pay off any debt they had. Maggie was able to keep it together, until after Tom returned to Arkansas. Once alone, and sure to be undisturbed, she fell apart. She didn't leave the room John died in for two weeks. Maggie was so scared of what the future held. She grappled with her identity.

She thought, "Without John what will become of me?"

She felt so helpless and vulnerable, but was the most overcome by sadness that could not be explained. Maggie hoped Tom couldn't see the huge rip in her armor. She had been so careful to maintain the facade of strength for years. After watching her mother be held captive by depression, Maggie vowed to never surrender to emotions that made her feel weak, until now.

Maggie's strong man facade was now coming apart at the seams, yet she didn't have the energy to sop up the sadness that gushed out of her. Maggie was lonely, but knew if she told Tom he would feel obligated to take care of her, so she managed.

Nevertheless, the peace that was supposed to come from being relieved of a burden never came. The hospital staff told Maggie that after John died, she could live her life again. They were wrong; Maggie was unable to live in total peace without her husband.

Granted, Maggie no longer heard the whirr of machines in Johns room, and it was quiet if that's what they meant, but being at peace with John's absence never materialized.

She even asked God, "Am I doing something wrong?"

But in her spirit God would answer, "I never said I would take your pain away, I only promised to be with you in that pain. My grace is sufficient in that, over time I will help you manage that pain."

At last, she acknowledged that nothing would replace the piece of her that John took with him when he died. Maggie knew that if she was going to live again, she'd have to learn how to function on what was left.

The Methodist Church that she faithfully attended was really good about checking on Maggie during the week. Some of the ladies would car pool, and pick her up for church. Maggie was very active in that church after John passed away. The members of that church treated Maggie like she was part of their family. Maggie became known as the "Church Grandma" to all the troubled teenagers in the area.

Her house was alive again. Although Maggie was not blessed with biological grandchildren, she still filled the grandmothers' role for a mess load of kids throughout the years. Even after all she had suffered, Maggie knew that God was still looking after her. God was providing joy for her previous sorrows. Her home was filled with the laughter of children again. Maggie was truly grateful that God was using her to console other people in tears.

Maggie was amazed that God would use someone like her, so scared by tragedy, as a tool to mend other broken hearts.

7

PANDORA'S BOX

For as long as Maggie had been a resident at Grandview Nursing Home, she couldn't recall having such an active mind. Exposure to these recent memories caused Maggie to question all of her prior relationships, but specifically her intimate bond with God.

Maggie wondered, "Have I kept everyone at a distance, including God? Did my experience at St. Anthony's scar me, and cause a portion of my heart to become unreachable?"

At that moment she realized that giving up her baby marked a loss of innocense. Maggie had constructed a wall to guard her heart, consequently, pushing everyone away. Losing her youngest son Charlie added another layer to harden her heart.

John's death signified the final brick that was to completely entomb her heart and soul. Maggie never allowed herself to fully grieve over any of those losses. Instead, she stuffed the sadness further inside, and out of sight.

Maggie's inner-life was somehow changed, and less colorful. Maggie closed off a piece of her heart, with every person she lost. Maggie thought that being strong meant turning off emotions. Indirectly, she was taught that wallowing in self pity gets a person nowhere. Besides, Maggie was able to ignore depressing thoughts, while ministering to the troubled kids in her community.

She thought, "My outer-life and good deeds really served God, while my inner-life and thoughts actually ran from Him!"

Everything seemed much clearer in hindsight, but Maggie was still confused about the specific timing of her clarity. Looking back, Maggie could see that if she had dealt with the mounting sadness earlier, then it wouldn't have gotten so big. The bulk of Maggie's sadness now threatened to consume her completely.

She wondered, "Why now am I more aware of my surroundings, along with a depth of insight that scares me?"

The only possible explanation had to be that she was dying. Maggie's life was flashing right before her eyes. Although this thought panicked Maggie, she still had a tiny bit of hope left that God might help her tie up some loose ends before she died.

The more thought Maggie gave to her last mission in life, the more impossible it seemed.

She thought, "How can I find my daughter if I can't talk?"

The only people who knew about Maggie's teenage pregnancy were her parents and John. Unfortunately, those three people were all dead. Then, Maggie thought about her son Tom, but remembered not seeing him since he had abandoned her at Grandview Nursing Home. Even if Tom would come for a visit, it would be impossible to communicate. Out of steam, and discouraged, Maggie nearly gave up. However, Maggie recalled her ability to wiggle a few fingers, and wondered if she could hold a pen to write.

In the distance, Maggie could hear the cafeteria come alive with activity. The clinking and clanking of plates signaled dinner time. This brought Maggie back to her memory of working the fields with her brother Avery. They would work until their mother rang the dinner bell. She was fascinated with the way a sound could trigger a memory from so long ago.

Maggie was intrigued by the power of human senses. The concept of how a present sight, sound, or a smell could cause a person experience a different time and place was mind boggling.

Maggie thought, "Too bad Albert Einstein never made time travel more than a theory. Otherwise, I could have altered my bad memories all together."

She thought, "Well maybe I'm not that far gone if I can still find humor in my own misfortunes."

Julie rolled the dinner cart into Maggie's room.

Julie announced with pride, "Tonight's special is fresh water trout with a side of brussels sprouts!"

With a hint of sarcasm in her voice, Priscilla replied, "Oh I can hardly contain myself!"

Julie's face fell. Maggie felt bad for Julie, but did agree with Priscilla that the fish was nothing to get excited about. Grandview's fresh water trout was rubbery in texture, and bland. Overall, the whole meal was just an unpleasant experience.

"And brussels sprouts," Priscilla said, "Gees, we may be close to death, but our taste buds still work!"

Maggie was starting to like Priscilla because she would say all the things that Maggie thought, but couldn't say. After Maggie managed to choke down mashed up fish and brussels sprouts, she figured it was time to get back to work on her plan. Getting a pen and paper was easy. What to write if she was successful was the hard part. Then she remembered praying for Priscilla, and how God answered that prayer. So Maggie closed her eyes, and prayed.

Maggie petitioned God with her thoughts, and prayed, "Dear God, it's Maggie again, I need you to make it possible to reach out to my son Tom, and to find my daughter, but most importantly when you pull this off, I need you to give me the strength to face them. Amen"

Maggie felt it was so important to receive her daughter's forgiveness before she died. Forgiveness from her daughter for not being the mother to love and raise her. Maggie wasn't sure why Tom never came to see her, but that didn't matter as long as God would fix it. She realized that what she was asking of God was a miracle, but at this point she was desperate.

Somehow after praying, Maggie had such an indescribable amount of peace come over her. She also had an extra measure of faith that God would come through. She just knew, beyond any of her own understanding, that God had heard her. Maggie trusted God to answer. The very peace that was at work in Maggie also had an effect on the atmosphere surrounding her.

Priscilla knew that Maggie couldn't speak or move, but she asked her a question anyway.

Priscilla asked, "Hey Mag, did you feel that, isn't it like our whole room has been swaddled in a warm blanket?"

At that moment Maggie realized just how far

God was reaching. God was reaching, not only to Maggie, but to Priscilla also! They both fell asleep early that night. A flash of bright light, and the loud crash of thunder startled Maggie from her peaceful slumber. The crackling rumble of thunder still rang fresh in her ears, as she noticed the reaction of her body. Even before her mind had the chance to process the loud noise, her startled body definitely jumped!

Much like an infant reacts to a sudden piercing sound, Maggie's arms and legs shot out as if trying to keep from falling off a cliff. This was so unusual because her body hadn't even twitched in years. Now her body was having a knee jerk reaction. Maggie struggled to move any part of her body again, but all she could wiggle was the right thumb and index finger. However, feeling the movement of her muscles again, if not but for a fleeting moment, was enough to give Maggie loads of hope.

Unable to go back to sleep, Maggie watched the shadows dance along the walls, and ceiling. Maggie remembered being a fearful little girl when it came to bad weather. Maggie's mother would comfort her by telling them not to be unsettled by a thunderstorm, because thunder was predictable.

Their mother would go on to say, "Lightning is a precursor to thunder, Gods little way of warning us to cover our ears!"

Even though Maggie thought her mothers explanation was a little far reaching, it served its purpose of calming her and Avery. The light quickly retreated from the room, and back to the heavens that sent it. Following the beautiful light show was only the sound of the sonic boom. Constant patter of rain was hypnotic, but a strike of lightning broke any trance. Thunder reminded Maggie how small she was compared to the rest of God's universe.

Maggie was fascinated by the way darkness seemed to chase after the light, which spontaneously lit up her room. As hard as the shadow tried; it was never able to grab hold of the light, or even get close to it. That little illustration caused Maggie to wonder if she, like the darkness, had chased the light, yet failed to get close enough. All those years of participating in church worship, and claiming to be a follower of Christ. Maggie believed she had a spot reserved in Heaven based solely on all her effort. Now she wondered it any of that mattered.

She thought, "Earning my salvation in all the good things I have done, may have added up to diddly squat."

Maggie had seen herself groping blindly for God through her works, and thinking she could make up for all of her mistakes. All the while God was right there beside her waiting for acknowledgment. He was knocking at the locked door of her heart. In a still small voice God was communicated to her. However, Maggie was never ready to listen to what He had to say.

She knew that God would require access to her pain. It was facing the hurt, and surrendering the right to be angry. To expose the ugliness of all she had suffered. Opening the door of her heart meant she had to trust God completely.

As long as Maggie was in control, she felt strong, and she usually found strength in the silence of all emotions. Maggie was afraid of opening the pandora's box of feelings because they would spill out all over the place. Once Maggie's emotions were in the open, she would no longer be able to manage them. So, she never found enough courage to open that door and lose control.

Instead of falling prey to emotions, Maggie just got better at staying busy. Maggie figured that if she could keep moving, then she could drown out that still small voice. Though the years, Maggie believed that she had it all together. In reality, she was actually running away from God, so that he wouldn't take her all apart.

With more irony than Maggie cared for, she finally accepted that she could no longer run from the things that hurt. That still small voice of Christ suddenly became loud and clear with a captive audience of one!

Watching the storm, and thinking of her mother's theory on thunder reminded Maggie of how much she missed her mom. When her mother died Tom came to Texas, and drove Maggie in for the funeral. There were not many people at her mother's funeral, but that didn't seem to bother anyone. Maggie and Tom sat beside her father during the funeral. Avery sat with Vivian and their daughter Ann. Ann's husband, Danny, and their four kids sat on the pew behind them.

Seeing her father break down was hard on Maggie. He'd been the strong one that held their family together, when Maggie's mother was too depressed to get out of bed.

Maggie finally understood the resentment she harbored for her mother. She had to admit that she had not truly forgiven her mother for forcing her to give up the baby, or for being absent due to depression. Maggie regretted not ever confronting the issue with her mother, but she never felt like the time was right.

She thought about talking to her father, but it seemed inappropriate to confront him, while he grieved the death of his wife. Maggie was glad that Tom was there to take care of her father. Instead of starting a family, Tom found contentment in being his grandfather's care giver. Maggie's father was preparing Tom to take over the farm when he died.

Maggie stayed a couple of days with Tom and her father after the funeral. Avery and his wife Vivian also stayed a night in their child hood home. Maggie was happy for Avery. After all, his wife was still alive, and he was a grandparent, but she still felt sorry for herself. She was just a little envious.

Maggie loved her family, but was sort of relieved when she got back home. She and John had started their own life in Texas. Even though Texas was where she'd lost her husband and son Charlie; it was also where they were put to rest. So, she felt like Texas was her home now. Oddly, living in the log cabin that John built with his own hands, made her feel closer to him.

When Maggie was missing Charlie, she would go upstairs, lay in his bed, and cuddle his favorite teddy bear. She would imagine what he was doing in heaven at that moment, and wished so badly to be there with him.

Most of the time though, Maggie kept busy doing whatever was needed for the community through her church. When John died she had to find another reason to live. Maggie needed a new purpose in life, and what she found brought her great joy.

Maggie realized that bringing hope to the hopeless was her new calling, and had been reaching out to hurting people ever since then. Sometimes all she could offer was a shoulder to cry on, or a hot meal, but everyone that she'd helped seemed grateful.

Three years after her mother's funeral, Maggie received a call from Tom. He informed her that, at age eighty-two, her father suffered a massive stroke. Luckily he died in his sleep and didn't suffer. Tom showed up the next day, and drove Maggie back to Berryville, Arkansas. Waves of anger and sadness washed over Maggie as she looked down at her father's casket. Anger because she remembered how losing John had caused so much fear and anxiety. And sadness as Maggie recalled seeing her fourteen-year-old son in his casket wearing the suit that her parents bought him.

Maggie thought, "I'm not sure I can handle another funeral."

Maggie had Tom bring her home the day after the funeral because she couldn't bear to be in that house one second longer. When Maggie got home, she tried to go back to her active life, but it seemed that she had lost a step. Slowly at first, Maggie started forgetting little things. One day Maggie forgot that she was running bath water, and flooded the bathroom downstairs. The pastor convinced her to tell Tom.

Of course, Tom was worried. He tried to talk Maggie into selling the cabin, and moving back to Arkansas. Maggie became defensive because she felt like her independence was being threatened.

Maggie sternly told her son, "Tom, your father built this house just for me, and this is where I will die!"

Tom replied, "Mama, I know that you love the house daddy built you, but I would never forgive myself if something bad happened."

Maggie's tone softened as she replied, "I know Tom, but just not now."

As Maggie hung up the phone, she knew that

was a mistake. She wondered whether or not telling Tom was a good idea. She suffered a little anxiety at the thought of losing her independence, but figured at least she wouldn't be so lonely all the time. Maggie knocked the idea around a few days, but decided that moving back to Arkansas was not what she wanted to do.

Maggie noticed that her room at Grandview was silent, and it was no longer raining outside, so she fell asleep. Maggie slipped into a dream where she saw John making repairs to the roof on their log cabin. Tom and Charlie were young boys in her dream. They were running around the yard playing cowboys and Indians. When John looked up at her, his foot slipped, and he fell off the house. About that time Tom, who was dressed as the Indian, shot a flaming arrow into the front door of their cabin. Maggie searched frantically for John, but couldn't find him. She realized that Charlie, dressed as a cowboy, was screaming from inside the burning house. Maggie woke up gasping for air. She pinched the bed sheet tightly between her thumb and index finger.

Maggie was able to calm herself down by thinking, "That didn't really happen, it was just a bad dream."

8

CONFRONTED WITH REALITY

That disturbing image of Maggie's home on fire was burned into her brain. Maggie's nightmare forced her to recall how she'd gotten from her home in Texas to Grandview Nursing Home in Arkansas.

Maggie was on the hospitality committee at church. She had agreed to fry all of the chicken at her house because the stove in the church's fellowship hall wasn't working. They had planned to host dinner at the local homeless shelter.

As Maggie placed pre battered chicken in the boiling grease, she heard something milling around outside of her home. Maggie's search for clues only led her farther away from home.

By the time Maggie looked up, she didn't

recognize her surroundings anymore. Panic set in, and Maggie couldn't remember how she got outside, or where she was. Maggie was confused, but managed to walk three miles in the dark before a church member recognized her. He pulled over, but eventually had to call the police because she would not get in his truck.

When Officer Terry got there, he convinced Maggie to let him drive her home. As they got closer to Maggie's house, it became obvious that the log cabin was on fire, and that was what illuminated the night sky! Maggie was horrified.

She asked, "What happened to my house?"

Officer Terry responded, "Don't you worry Mrs. Maggie, we will find out what happened, but right now I'm gonna get you to the hospital, so they can make sure you're not hurt!"

After getting Maggie admitted, Officer Terry called Tom to tell him the news. The next day, Tom traveled to Memorial Hospital to visit his mother.

Maggie asked him, "Is it still standing?"

He replied, "It's unliveable, so you're going back to Arkansas with me, and that's final!"

Maggie was shocked. Tom had never spoken to her like that before. She didn't argue.

She thought, "He must be really mad!"

Tom and Avery had arranged a welcome home party for Maggie. Among all the chaos, something familiar brought her comfort. Vivian baked a cake. Ann and her kids decorated the old farm house with streamers and balloons. Maggie wasn't too crazy about living in her dead parent's house, but it did have a homy quality. The whole family reassured Maggie that they would be visiting really often, and that everything was gonna be okay.

Somebody in her family came by daily to bring food, or to just watch televison. Avery's grandchildren were over most of the time, and Maggie loved it because it was like having grand kids of her own. Maggie also got really close to Avery's wife Vivian, and wondered how she ever disliked her. Ann was really good at coming by too, but she reminded Maggie too much of the baby she gave up.

Everything seemed to be going well, until the day that Tom found Maggie wandering around outside naked. She became increasingly fearful, forgetful, and hostile. Maggie was diagnosed with Alzheimer's disease, and Tom was forced to seek out long term care.

She remembered the terrifying day Tom brought her to Grandview Nursing Home. All of Maggie's fears were now solidified, and staring her right in the face. She knew then that her life was over, and she would die in that nursing home alone! Maggie was sure her family would just forget about her.

She thought, "Out of sight, out of mind!"

In the years after John died, Maggie would visit the old folks home with the church. She felt sorry for those old people because there was an expression of hopelessness on every face. Their eyes spoke of great sadness. Tom got Maggie admitted as a permeant resident. Maggie feared that she would now join the sea of hopeless faces.

Maggie's old worn out brain could remember only so much, and she went blank. Early that morning, right before the sun came up, Maggie could feel someone massaging her leg.

Some old man said, "Hello, baby!"

Maggie let out a scream that woke Priscilla. Priscilla jumped out of her bed, and started hitting the old man with her pillow.

Priscilla screamed, "Julie, come quick, there's a dirty old man molesting Maggie!"

Julie ran in, and flipped the light switch.

Julie shrieked, "Mr. Earl Jenkins, what are you doing? You'd better get on out of here."

With a dirty grin, Earl said, "My name is Earl, but my buddies call me Gator!"

Maggie gagged and nearly vomited.

She thought, "You have got to be kidding me, this dirty old man can't be Gator, as in the father of my baby!"

Maggie was mortified. She heard Julie telling Priscilla that Mr. Jenkins was the newest resident at Grandview Nursing Home. After Julie shooed Gator back to his room, she assured Maggie that wouldn't happen again. A little while later it was time to eat. Breakfast smelled like apple cinnamon oatmeal, one of Maggie's favorites. Right behind that steaming bowl of oatmeal was nurse Julie's smiling face.

Julie commented, "Your brother Avery told me you like apple cinnamon oatmeal, so I thought I'd surprise you!"

Maggie looked around the room.

She wondered, "Who's Avery?"

Julie could tell she was confused, so she changed the subject.

Julie commented, "It's awfully pretty today!"

Smiling, Julie asked, "How would you like to go outside for a little while after breakfast?"

Maggie's eyes got big, and she smiled.

Julie said, "I'll take that as a yes!"

Julie put Maggie in her wheel chair, and rolled her outside. It felt so good to breathe in some fresh air, and see the color that nature had brought. Maggie was pleasantly surprised by the sight of falling leaves, the sound of rustling leaves, and the smell of fall. Maggie could feel the cool crisp breeze blowing through her long gray hair. Being surrounded by the beauty of fall brought her a sense of contentment. Maggie suddenly understood that her time was nearly up, and soon she'd be reunited with John and Charlie. Julie sat with Maggie in silence for along time holding her hand, and admiring fall's beautiful colors. It was almost lunch time, so Julie rolled Maggie back to her room. Julie brought in chicken noodle soup, but Maggie was too tired to eat, so she just went to sleep.

As soon as Maggie fell into a deep sleep, her brain was ablaze with activity. Maggie wasn't sure if she was dreaming, or dead because all of the sudden she could see nothing, and all was black with no end in sight. The darkness was suffocating, as it gripped her very soul. There was no floor to the abyss that Maggie now found herself in.

The mood of that dark place was far beyond despair, and much like a kind of sorrow that paralyzed a person. The place smelled old and musty. Another whiff smelled of sulfur and death, which completely infiltrated Maggie's nostrils. Maggie couldn't tell if she was at the door of her heart of the entrance of Hell.

Maggie couldn't see anything, but what she heard was enough to utterly terrify her. Both near and far were the screams of pain, agony, and torment. Those were just a few that Maggie recognized. It felt as though fear itself had coiled itself around her body. Similar to the way a python squeezes the life out of its prey; fear's grip got tighter around her, and death came a little closer. Maggie was certain that she had only one breath left, and there was only one name that could save her.

With little strength left, she managed to whisper, "Jesus."

However, nothing happened immediately.

Maggie thought, "This is it! I'm doomed!"

Just as she was about to close her eyes, and

give into death, Maggie saw a projection screen light up. She could see a man sitting in a chair, and facing the screen. It looked as if he was watching home videos. In the first scene there was a cute sleeping baby. Next, was a baby eating spaghetti, and then something like first steps. These home videos featured some highlights in life. The movies captured the first day of school, and first Christmas. The man watching seemed delighted. At times he would affectionately laugh because of a cute expression.

Maggie figured the man knew that little girl because of the way he studied her gestures. She figured it was the father of that girl in the way he watched her. The little girl grew into a young lady, and experienced first communion. Then Maggie noticed a change in the man's posture, as if he was no longer enjoying the film. She looked back at the screen to see why this man was now sad. In this scene there was a young girl giving birth to a baby. Maggie watched in horror, as it became clear that she was the star of this film. She wanted to run, but she couldn't move.

Maggie wanted to scream for the film to stop, but she couldn't speak. Maggie tried to close her eyes, or look away, but something kept her eyes focused on that screen. She could do nothing, but watch her life spiral downward. Maggie was being forced to experience every emotion associated with those events. As each dreadful event unfolded, another brick was removed from the wall that guarded her heart.

Her pain was atrocious, yet no detail was left out. The following frame to flash on a screen was her son Charlie in a casket. Maggie felt as if she was being pulled from the inside out. Every bit of pain from that horrible day flooded her soul. She begged for death, and an end to this torture. The man rose from his chair, turned, and walked toward Maggie. At first glance, Maggie was truly captivated by what glory she saw in his eyes.

As He got closer, Maggie could see an expression of sorrow on his face, and now more visible were the many trails of dried tears.

He gently cradled Maggie's face.

The man said, "Maggie Ann, you're almost there, and I promise this is for your own good."

Maggie was at a loss of words.

She thought, "How does this man know my name, my life, or what's good for me?"

As this man let go of her face, Maggie could see holes in both of his hands. Immediately she recognized this man to be Jesus Christ, the Son of God. Before she could get lost in his presence, the screen flashed another scene. It was her oldest son lying in the hospital bed. Tom was in a coma. She and John were discussing how to tell Tom about Charlie.

Maggie asked, "How is Tom going to cope with being responsible for Charlie's death?"

Then Maggie noticed a tear fall from Tom's

eye. She had never realized the possibility that Tom could hear their conversation. This realization brought Maggie a tremendous amount of guilt. Maggie wanted to hide, but there was no where to go. Maggie thought it was impossible to feel any more misery, when a flicker of film flashed on a screen. It was her husband John, as he lay dying. Seeing that was like taking a punch to the gut leaving Maggie absent of air.

Despair crept back in, and hopelessness nearly swallowed her. Maggie recalled old feelings of helplessness, as she watched cancer slowly consume John. Suicidal thoughts ran through her mind. Far worse, was that the film ended with the log cabin that John built her on fire! Emotionally and physically Maggie was brought to her knees. The last brick from her wall of protection was blown away.

Jesus helped Maggie up, and embraced her.

He said, "I have seen you suffer, and I have heard your cry, but I have never left you."

He went on to say, "Come and rest in me. With the many colors of your loss, I will paint a beautiful picture."

Maggie woke up the next morning unable to stop crying. With each gut wrenching sob Maggie was finding it harder to breathe. Her loud sobs woke Priscilla, and she noticed Maggie was having trouble breathing.

So Priscilla screamed, "Help she's dying!"

In order to calm Maggie down a nurse decided

to give her a tranquilizer shot. After Maggie stopped crying, she noticed a roomful of people gawking at her, and was completely embarrassed. Julie brought in meatloaf for dinner, but Maggie refused to eat. Julie didn't push because she knew that Maggie was preparing for death. Maggie just wanted to disappear, so she closed her eyes pretending to sleep. It seemed to have worked because she could hear their voices go to a murmur, as they cleared the room.

Maggie thought about her dream. She had never experienced anything quite like that before. She decided that it was God speaking to her through a dream. Before Maggie had much more time to think about her dream, the priest walked in, and sat down.

About that time Priscilla spouted off, "Well Father, it's a good thing you're here because Maggie almost died this morning!"

Luckily, Julie was standing in the hall, and over heard their conversation. She poked her head in Maggie's room.

Julie said, "Now that's not entirely true, Maggie just woke up crying, and we gave her something to relax."

The priest said, "Oh I see, well Priscilla I'll bet Maggie sure is proud to have a friend like you looking out for her."

Priscilla smiled proudly.

She replied, "Yeah well what are friends for?"

The priest opened his bible to the gospel of

John, and read through to the second chapter, then closed with a prayer.

It was obvious, something in the scripture reached out to Priscilla because she asked, "Do you hear confessions?"

He answered, "Yes, I do."

Priscilla responded, "Sometimes when my son, and his wife come to visit me, I truly don't recognize them, but most of the time I do. And those times I do recognize them, I act as if I don't know who they are, but the reason is because I can tell I'm getting worse, and eventually I really won't recognize my son at all. So, simply because I'm humiliated to think that he will see me slowly lose all ability to function, I'd rather just let him go now."

The priest replied, "Have you discussed this with your son and his wife?"

Priscilla said, "Heck no, that would blow my cover!"

The priest said, "It might be beneficial to be transparent with your son, so he can understand how you feel. Then, your family can come to some reasonable compromise, or agreement for future visits."

There was a knock at the door, and in walked Priscilla's son and wife.

Priscilla shouted, "Speak of the devil!"

Carefully they approached her bed, and Priscilla smiled.

She said, "I have something to say to you two, I'm sorry that sometimes I act like I don't recognize you in order to save face, but I now realize that I may be doing more harm than good."

She paused then grabbed her daughter-in-law's hand.

Priscilla said, "Ann, I'm sorry I hit you with a pudding cup, and called you a hooker. That's not true, you are the best thing that has happened to my son Danny!"

Priscilla hugged both Danny and Ann, and told them how much she loved them. It was getting late, so Priscilla's son and daughter-in-law said goodbye. As they were walking out to leave, Ann gave the priest a big hug.

Ann said, "Thank you for all you're doing."

She then gave Maggie a hug.

Softly Ann said, "Aunt Maggie, it's Ann, I'm your brother Avery's little girl, you may not remember me, but that's okay. I just wanted to say I love you."

The priest told Maggie he'd see her tomorrow, and they all started to walk out together. Maggie was stunned mainly because Priscilla was right. Maggie's niece Ann had married Priscilla's son Danny. However, Maggie couldn't remember what Ann's face looked like. Maggie hadn't even given thought to the fact that she had a brother, who may still be alive.

Panic began to surge through Maggie's mind and body as she thought, "There must be a conspiracy brewing!"

Maggie peered suspiciously at the priest, as he waved goodbye to her and Priscilla.

A few minutes later Maggie heard a nurse yell, "lights out!"

Exhausted Maggie went to sleep rather quickly. She dreamed that she was in a large wheat field with a single massive weeping willow tree in the center. Maggie watched how the field of wheat responded to each gust of wind. She was in a state of peace and tranquility, as the gentle breeze caressed Maggie's skin. She closed her eyes, and became one with the harmonious rhythm. Hearing birds chirping, prompted Maggie to move closer to that sizeable weeping willow tree in the center. Standing under its monolithic covering Maggie knew that she was safe. It felt like she could stay there forever.

Morning had arrived to wake Maggie from her dream. She was not happy because she'd planned on not waking up, but some how Maggie's plans never seemed to work out. Julie brought in breakfast, but she no longer wore a smile. Instead Julie looked like she was grieving someone's death.

Again, Maggie refused to eat. Julie sat on Maggie's bed, and held her hand.

Julie said, "Your son has arranged to take you home with hospice care. I know you're ready, but I'm still sad to see you go. I have grown fond of you, and will miss you badly."

Maggie thought, "They're sending me home to die!"

In tears, Julie continued, "Your son said he'd be here before lunch to get you."

Maggie was moved by Julie's emotional attachment to her. Maggie wanted to say something nice, but she could only whimper. Julie must have understood because she hugged Maggie for a long time, then left.

From across the room Priscilla said, "I bet I know who's gonna do your funeral!"

Then she got up, and shuffled over to Maggie's bed.

She said, "Well old gal, it's been fun knowing you. I hope you can forgive me for how I acted at Ann and Danny's wedding."

She went on to say, "When you get to heaven do me a favor, and find Grandma Harrison. Tell her I love her and will see her soon."

She kissed Maggie on the cheek.

Priscilla said, "Thanks."

Then got back in her bed. Maggie fell asleep.

9

SENT HOME WITH HOSPICE

She was awakened by the priest's voice. He was talking to Julie.

Maggie thought, "Well looks like I'll get to see the priest before going home."

She was able to make out what they were saying.

Julie said to the priest, "Father, I was born at St. Anthony's Home for Unwed Mothers in 1945."

Julie then asked, "Can you tell me how to go about obtaining records on a closed adoption, and finding my birth mother?"

The priest replied, "I'll get the phone number to St. Anthony's, and bring it back up here when I get my mother settled in. When you call, tell them that Father Tom Anderson referred you. They should be able to help you."

The priest walked in Maggie's room.

He asked, "Mama, are you ready to go home?"

Maggie was astonished by this revelation; the priest was her son Tom. Maggie was sure that she heard him say that his name was Father Tom Anderson. Then, the priest walked in her room, and called her mama! All these years, she'd thought that Tom had just abandoned her, and left her there to die, but she was wrong. The paramedics transferred Maggie from her adjustable bed to the metal stretcher with wheeled legs. As Maggie was being wheeled out, she could see that Priscilla was sitting on her bed, and crying.

Maggie said, "Goodbye, my old friend."

Priscilla jumped from her bed, and ran to Maggie's bed.

Priscilla said, "She remembers me!"

Priscilla hugged Maggie. The staff loaded Maggie up in an ambulance, and Tom jumped in the back to sit with her for a short ride home. Maggie stared at Tom's face the whole way home trying to place him in her memory.

Soon Maggie's fear led to panic.

She thought, "How could I not remember my son, or the fact that he's a priest?"

She continued to scan her memory bank, but came up with nothing.

Maggie wondered, "What has happened to my

brain?"

Everything that Maggie thought was real, and concrete were, in fact, not stable at all. An enormous wave of confusion washed over her.

Maggie thought, "Where are they taking me, and why are they moving me?"

As her anxiety rose with her heart beat, and her breathing became labored.

Tom said, "Mama, it's okay we're just going home."

Then, the paramedic put an oxygen mask over Maggie's mouth, and said, "Just try to relax."

They arrived at the old farm house, wheeled her out, and down the front sidewalk. Maggie saw a man standing against a tree in front of their house.

As Maggie was wheeled past the man, he said, "Hey, my sweet sister, I'm glad you're home."

Maggie recognized his voice to be that of her brother Avery, but he looked much older than she remembered. After Tom got Maggie set up in the sick room, her whole family came in to visit. At first Maggie didn't recognize one single face, which scared her badly.

But then Ann walked up and said, "Hi Aunt Maggie, it's Ann, your niece."

Immediately, She remembered what Priscilla had told her, and recalled being at Ann and Danny's wedding. Then, Maggie remembered who officiated their wedding, and he looked a lot like the Priest who had been visiting her at Grandview Nursing Home. She even recalled approaching the priest before Ann's wedding to hug him, and congratulate her son Tom on his first wedding.

Maggie felt pitiful, as she wondered, "How could something that important ever slip my mind?"

Still unsure about her surroundings, Maggie looked around grasping for anything she recognized. Then, her eyes landed on a picture of her mother and father. Feeling more safe and secure Maggie carefully examined the faces that surrounded her. She experienced such love and acceptance.

Maggie thought, "Well maybe I did do some good after all."

Maggie's mood went from euphoria to dysphoria, as she thought of the daughter she never met. While at Grandview Nursing Home, Julie sat with Maggie outside. She had finally accepted dying, and made peace with herself, but now was having reservations.

Maggie thought, "I will not leave this earth without finding my daughter! Heaven can wait!"

Maggie could feel something within her soul being stirred with a restless excitement. Apparently, Tom could tell something was going on, and he asked their family come back later, so Maggie could get some rest.

Tom walked out with them, and turned the lights out.

He said, "Mom, you try and get some rest, Uncle Avery's is going to stay with you, while I bring something to the nursing home, I'll be back soon."

Left alone with only her thoughts, and God, Maggie experienced all kinds of emotions. Regret that she waited too long to find her daughter. Frustration because her body was useless, and her mind was, at the moment, working so well it was torture. Maggie harbored anger at God, herself, Gator, and the situation. Sadness, because she worried about the family she was leaving behind, especially her daughter.

Maggie thought, "If my daughter wants to find me, but only finds my grave, then she'll have no closure."

Logically, Maggie realized that she had no right to be angry with God, but it was like her heart didn't know any better.

Maggie often thought, "Well if God wanted to intervene, He could've changed my mother's mind, or prevented me from even meeting Gator. God could've caused me and my daughter to cross paths, but he did not!"

Maggie wondered why she didn't stand up to her mother, Sister Agnus, and society to fight for her baby. In tears now Maggie considered the possibility that maybe she was weak, and all those years, pretending to be strong was only running from a truth. She was just like her mother.

Maggie realized that her whole life revolved around working so hard to be opposite of her mother. Any time things went wrong enough to cry about, she refused weakness, stuffed emotions, and was strong for everyone else. Maggie feared that if she sat in misery too long, she'd end up just like her mother, and would be lost forever. But now looking back, Maggie understood that she had missed out on just simply being herself, which brought extreme sadness.

Avery walked in and said, "Don't cry my little sister, it's all gonna be okay."

He sat by the bed, held her hand, and stroked her hair. Maggie was comforted with having her big brother there.

In tears Avery said, "Well I told myself to be strong for you. I wasn't going to let you see me cry, but I'm just not strong like you. I'm gonna miss you!"

Maggie began to cry, and Avery hugged her.

He said, "I'm sorry I wasn't there for you more. That first Thanksgiving after I left for the military, I could tell something was wrong, but didn't ask, and I'm sorry."

Maggie saw her chance to make it right, so she struggled to get Avery's attention, and say something about finding her daughter. Maggie began brainstorming on how to tell Avery in a few words what was wrong. Maggie was going to tell him why she was sad that day. That it was because she was pregnant. So, she opened her mouth, and pushed air through her voice box.

Maggie stammered, "I, I, I, I, was, was, was . . . "

Excited, Avery jumped up, and put his ear closer to Maggie's mouth.

He asked, "You were what?"

Maggie tried again to speak, but to no avail. She gave up to pure exhaustion. Moments later Tom arrived back from the nursing home. Avery walked outside.

Avery said, "Maggie was trying to tell me something, but she couldn't finish."

Tom ran into Maggie's sick room.

He said, "Its okay mama."

Tom fell on his knees and prayed the Lords Prayer. Then prayed, "God, please give my mother peace, and comfort with your Holy Spirit in Jesus' name, Amen."

When Tom opened his eyes, he saw that Maggie was sound a sleep, and she looked very peaceful. Maggie dreamed that she was walking from room to room in the old farm house looking for something. Maggie searched every room on the first floor, but didn't find what she was looking for. Even though it was unclear what exactly Maggie expected to regain, she kept searching. Maggie made her way up the stairs, and entered Avery's room. After shuffling though some of his things nothing caught her attention. Maggie walked out into the hall, and looked at the only room she hadn't looked through yet. It was her room, and for some reason Maggie was filled with anxiety, as she put her hand around the door knob.

Maggie pulled back with fear.

She thought, "What is in my room that would cause these negative emotions?"

Maggie stood staring at that closed door for a long time, but curiosity was beginning to trump her fear of the unknown. She twisted the door knob, and carefully pushed open the door. Her door made a creaking sound, and it startled her. Maggie was too far in to back out now, so she proceeded to walk in. Maggie's room looked just like it did when she was a little girl. She sat on her bed, and looked into the mirror. The woman in the mirror scared the mess out of her.

An old woman's face peered back at Maggie. Just as she decided to make a run for it something inside her said, "Relax, this is just your reflection."

She was able to collect herself, and grasp that the old woman was her face. Maggie walked closer to get a better look. Sure enough, it was her reflection.

She whispered, "My word, when did I get so wrinkled?"

As Maggie was pondering this question, she noticed something in the mirror. Something behind her was out of place. She turned around to get a better look at what caught her eye. Maggie picked it up. She recognized it to be the lap quilt that her mother had given her for Christmas the year she stayed at St. Anthony's Home for Unwed Mothers.

Maggie thought, "There's no way I am holding this because I remember giving this blanket to Sister Agnus for my daughter."

Maggie couldn't ignore the comfort she felt by holding this quilt. Maggie grabbed her teddy bear off the bed, and swaddled it in the quilt. She pretended it was her baby daughter, and she held it tight.

Maggie sang a hymn, "Turn your eye's upon Jesus."

That was the hymn she'd sang to Tom and Charlie when they were babies. Maggie sat back down on her bed, and spoke to the swaddled teddy bear all the things she had wanted to tell her daughter.

She said, "I have never forgotten you, and I'm sorry I wasn't there for you. Please find it in your heart to forgive me. Before dying I need to tell you that if I could go back, and change anything in my life, the one thing I would change was not keeping you."

Maggie reclined in her bed holding the teddy bear wrapped in the quilt, and fell asleep in her dream. Maggie opened her eyes, but knew she was still dreaming. Maggie was about to get up when she noticed something sticking out from under her mattress. She pulled it out, and realized that it was her old journal with the dirty napkin featuring Gator's phone number tucked inside. Maggie opened her journal, thumbed through the pages, and understood that in these pages were a detailed account of what went down at St. Anthony's.

Maggie heard voices, but wasn't sure if she was still dreaming or not. Upon coming to a more wakeful state, Maggie could still hear those same voices. She opened her eyes. Maggie could see Avery, Vivian, Ann, and Tom talking, and smiling as they looked through photo albums. Ann noticed that Maggie was awake, so she moved closer to her bed with the albums. Avery, Vivian, Ann and Tom were now showing pictures to Maggie, and giggling about childhood stories. Pictures of Avery and Maggie at Christmas showing off their apples and oranges.

One picture was of Maggie and Avery standing in the tree house they built. Another picture was of Maggie's sixteenth birthday wearing her first store-bought dress. Then, Ann flipped to the family picture taken at Thanksgiving. That was the year Maggie found out she was pregnant.

Tom said, "Wow mom looked so sad in this picture."

Avery said, "Yeah I remember that Thanksgiving, and how sad Maggie looked, but I never got around to asking her what was wrong."

Maggie was whimpering as she remembered the dream she just had. She knew if she could tell them to go get that diary under her mattress, then they would know. Maggie tried to talk but all she could utter was a grunting noise. Getting her second wind, Maggie focused all of her strength and energy. Somehow she was able to raise her arm, and point upstairs toward her bedroom.

Maggie whispered, "Diary."

But pulling off that task cost her greatly because she felt an enormous amount of pain in her shoulder. Maggie had torn a ligament. The pain was so extreme that it caused her to pass out. When Maggie came to, she cried out in agony. Luckily hospice care had already arrived, and was prepared with pain medication. The medicine brought some relief, but left a dull ache. She was getting groggy, but was fighting to stay awake. The hospice nurse asked Tom if she could give Maggie something to help her rest, and he agreed.

Maggie thought, "Oh no, I need to stay awake, and tell them about my daughter!"

But it was too late, the shot was given, and Maggie could fight sleep no more. Maggie dreamed of Julie, the nurse from Grandview Nursing Home, sitting outside with her.

While holding Maggie's hand Julie said, "I feel like we're connected, kindred spirits, I bet your children are so proud to have you as their mother."

Maggie turned to look at Julie and said, "It's weird, because I feel like we're connected too, but I'm no perfect mother, all mothers make mistakes."

After a brief pause Maggie said, "Tell me about your mother."

Julie replied, "Well the mother who raised me was a sweet, and tender woman who told me she loved me every day. The mother who gave birth to me I never got to meet."

Maggie answered in tears, "You should look for her before it's too late."

Maggie woke up sobbing, and Ann ran to her side.

Ann asked, "Aunt Maggie, are you okay, do you have any pain?"

While Maggie was crying, Ann wiped away her aunt's tears, and cried with her. She could see that Avery had something in his hand, as he approached Vivian to whisper in her ear. Maggie could see shock on Vivian's face when she looked at her. Vivian called the family into the other room.

Maggie could hear them talking.

Avery said, "Earlier when we were looking through pictures Maggie got excited, pointed up to her room, and said something like "diary". So I went upstairs to check it out. I looked everywhere a girl might hide a diary, and came up empty-handed. Then I remembered one time she stole my baseball card, and hid it under her mattress. I ran my hand under the mattress of her bed upstairs, and I found a diary."

There was a pause like they were reading. Maggie could hear the gasps of her family, and oddly enough that brought some relief.

Maggie thought, "My mother told me that I would bring this secret to the grave, but my mother was mistaken!"

A couple of seconds later someone rang the door bell, but Maggie drifted off before she could tell who it was. While Maggie was asleep, her family brought their visitor up to speed. Maggie awoke and spotted Julie, the nurse, speaking with the family. They were crying and hugging each other.

She was confused as she thought, "What is Julie from the nursing home doing at my house?"

She noticed a bouquet of flowers and a gift. Maggie realized that Julie must be there to pay her respects. When Tom noticed that Maggie was awake, he asked for everybody to clear the room, so Julie could talk to her. This sort of freaked Maggie out because she thought that Julie had news of maybe Priscilla dying or something. Julie was crying too hard to really say anything, so she just set down the flowers, and opened the gift she'd brought.

Julie unfolded a blanket.

She said, "Maggie, I got your address from St. Anthony's Home for Unwed Mothers because I was searching for my birth mother. I also brought this quilt that came home with me from the orphanage. I was told that my birth mother wanted me to have it."

Maggie looked at the quilt Julie held, and she recognized it to be the quilt her mother gave her for

Christmas.

Maggie thought, "Sister Agnus kept her promise!"

Julie went on to say, "Avery let me read your diary. I hope you don't mind, but I have gained the answers to all my questions!"

Maggie was overwhelmed with joy. She wanted to hug her daughter, and kiss every inch of her face. Julie must have known this because she held Maggie tightly for a long time.

Julie said, "I knew there was something different about you when I took care of you at the nursing home."

She went on to say, "I have never been mad at you for doing what you had to do. I had a great loving family raise me, and if I had known how you felt about me, I would have sought you out a lot sooner. I won't lose you again so, I'm staying here until the end, you will not die alone!"

Maggie prayed to herself, "God, thank you for keeping your eyes on me, but more than that, thank you for never leaving me even when I blamed you."

As Maggie studied Julie's face it became so clear. After all, she looked just like Maggie did at that age, red hair, green eyes, skinny, tall. Everything was falling in to place for Maggie to find closure, and to really be at peace with leaving this world. This emotional roller coaster Maggie had been on for the last week was really taking its toll because her body and mind were just worn out. She needed to rest her eyes, and prior to realizing it she went to sleep.

10

HEAVENLY DREAM REVEALED

It seemed like no time after Maggie had fallen asleep that she was dreaming again. Standing in a large doorway, Maggie looked around, and knew this was the same dream she had twice before. Maggie walked in, and her first stop was to see if Priscilla was still in the waiting room for Hell.

As Maggie passed by, she noticed that all those rooms were empty. With a sigh of relief, Maggie went straight for the stream. She hopped in, and realized that it was different this time. This time it was not fog, but water!

When Maggie reached the other side, and got out. She was soaking wet, but kept on going anyway. Maggie couldn't wait to get to Jesus, so when the

Angel of God appeared, she didn't stare so long. The little boy tripped, and Maggie picked him back up. When he looked up at her, Maggie suddenly realized that this little boy was her son Charlie!

Charlie smiled and said, "Thank you, mom." Then he hugged her and said, "I've missed you!"

Maggie held her son closely and said, "My baby I have missed you too, but I'm here now!"

Charlie turned to show her Jesus, and as in the other dreams, Jesus motioned for them to sit at a table. As they sat down, two open Bibles appeared, and from behind Jesus pointed at scripture. Maggie tried to be quicker at reading this time.

The scripture that Jesus was pointing to was "My grace is sufficient for you, for my strength is made perfect in weakness." That scripture, 2 Corinthians 12:9, was her favorite. And suddenly Maggie's whole life made perfect sense.

Yes, she suffered a lot, and had a right to be bitter, but instead she let God use her broken heart to heal others. Holding back tears, she locked eyes with Christ.

Jesus said, "Maggie Ann, are you ready to come home?"

Maggie replied, "Yes Lord, I am ready."

When Maggie woke up, she felt so full of peace, and so much lighter. Looking around the room, Maggie noticed that Julie was showing pictures to a lady with three children. There was also a man on the other side holding the hand of a little red headed girl. Julie, seeing that Maggie was awake, walked over and began to introduce everyone.

Julie said, "This is my daughter Mary and my grandchildren, Kevin, Alex, and Samantha."

Then she said, "This is my son James and his little girl Madison."

Julie turned to her kids and grandchildren.

Julie said, "This is my mother Maggie."

As each one of them hugged Maggie she thought, "All these years, I have been a real grandma and great grandma!"

Maggie had always imagined what grandchildren would feel like or if they would look and act like her. Every one of the girls had red hair. The boys were handsome, and polite. Maggie thought this life could offer nothing more than what she was dealt, but she was wrong.

Julie told Maggie about her wonderful life, how it felt to be a grandparent, and that she was happily married. She watched how Julie interacted with her children, and grandchildren as they recalled cherished moments. The life Julie had created for herself was so full of love and family.

Maggie was amazed at how God took Julie's life, which started out with such terrible loss, and made it something so beautiful.

Maggie could feel herself slipping further away. Tom was aware of this, and he stood beside her.

He said, "Everything is taken care of; it's okay to go."

As Tom stroked her hair, Maggie opened her eyes and said, "Son, I love you and thank you for taking care of me."

He hugged her and whispered, "I love you too, mom."

Maggie closed her eyes for the last time, and breathed her final breath with a room full of people who loved her. Tom arranged Maggie funeral service to be held at Berryville United Methodist Church in Arkansas. Berryville United Methodist Church was the church where she and John were married.

Tom was also able to convince Grandview Nursing Home to bring all able body residents who were impacted by Maggie's life. Tom called Maggie's pastor in Texas to tell him that she'd passed.

Pastor White said, "I'm so sorry, your mother was very special to me, and I'll miss her."

Tom replied, "Yes I understand that she touched a lot of people's lives in Texas, which brings me to my question."

Tom continued, "My mother's last wishes were to be buried in Texas next to Charlie, so would you be willing to do the grave side service?"

Pastor White answered, "I would be honored."

When Maggie's body arrived at Berryville United Methodist Church, Tom was able to spend some time alone with her before the service.

Tom knew that his mother was no longer in that body, but he still placed his hand over Maggie's and said, "Goodbye Mother, I know you're in a better place, no longer suffering, but it still hurts to see you go."

Tom sat there holding his mother's hand, and allowed himself to grieve. Although there was no one in that room except Maggie's body and Tom, he didn't feel alone. Tom felt the presence of the Holy Spirit unlike he had ever experienced. As Tom wept, he could sense someone holding him. Immediately in his spirit Tom knew that it was Jesus!

Although, Tom had seen nothing with his eyes, or heard anything with his ears, he was certain that Jesus was there crying with him, and saying, "You are not alone in suffering because I am always with you."

A sense of peace came over Tom. God filled him with enough strength to pull himself together, and comfort those present at Maggie's funeral. As people started showing up, Tom stood at the door to greet them. Avery walked in, and fell apart. Tom nearly lost it.

Luckily Vivian said, "Come on honey let's go sit down."

Ann and Danny escorted Priscilla, who thanked Tom for setting it up so that she and Maggie could be room mates at Grandview.

Ann said, “We are here for you, anything you need, please let us know.”

Tom nodded.

Julie walked in with her family.

Tom hugged her tight and said, “I’m sorry I didn’t know sooner, so that you could have spent more time with her.”

Julie replied, “Don’t worry about that because I believe that everything happens for a reason, so I am at peace.”

Tom smiled and responded, “Well you and I still have time to catch up, big sister.”

Julie said, “Yes we do.”

Julie walked over to sit with the rest of their family. A bunch of other folks that Tom didn’t know showed up, and some said they’d known Maggie in school, or from The Hillbilly Hoe Down. Grandview Nursing Home was nice enough to bus ten more residents for Maggie’s funeral. Maggie’s peers from Grandview all said that, even before she lost her ability to speak, she was still a good listener.

Before Tom knew it, the little sanctuary was full, and it was time to start Maggie’s funeral service. Tom made Julie and her family move up to sit between him and Avery.

Tom commented, “You are as much a part of this family as we are.”

Julie was so moved by the compassion Tom had shown her that she wept freely. Maggie’s funeral service started with a prayer for the friend's and family, then led into a scripture reading from second Corinthians chapter four, verse seven.

The Reverend read aloud, "But we have this treasure in earthen vessels, that the excellence of the power may be of God and not us. We are hard-pressed on every side, yet we are not crushed; we are perplexed, but not in despair. We are persecuted, but not forsaken. We are struck down, but not destroyed."

He continued, "We do not look at the things which are seen, but at the things which are not seen. For the things which are seen are temporary, but the things which are not seen are eternal."

Reverend White put his Bible down, and took his glasses off to address the crowd.

Reverend White said, "Today we celebrate the life of Maggie Ann Anderson."

He went on to say, "In life, Maggie experienced a lot of suffering, but no matter what came her way, she was determined to help someone else. She was the kind of person that you meet only once in a lifetime. God used Maggie to minister to so many hurting people over the years. There was such a glow about Maggie when she was serving other people. She was truly a reflection of Christ's heart. Maggie will be missed greatly, but we can honor her by following her example, and striving to have more of a servant's heart."

Reverend White closed with a prayer, then

everyone sang from the hymnal, "Turn your eyes upon Jesus."

After dismissal, Tom and Julie followed the hearse to Texas for Maggie's grave side service, and burial. Tom told Julie about Charlie on the trip over, and how Maggie had requested to be buried next to him. Upon arrival at Fairmont Cemetery in Texas, Tom was greeted by more people than he could count. He had no idea that his mom was so loved. The Methodist preacher did the grave side service.

Pastor Norton opened with prayer then moved onto the scripture reading which was second Corinthians chapter twelve, verse nine.

He said, "My grace is sufficient for you, for my strength is made perfect in weakness."

Then Pastor Norton said, "Today Maggie Ann Anderson is enjoying Heaven, surrounded by loved ones that have gone before her. Her husband John and her son Charlie have been waiting for this day to reunite with Maggie. Even though, we are sad to see Maggie go, we can be comforted in knowing that she is in a far better place than we are."

Pastor Norton paused, and wiped his eyes with a white handkerchief.

He continued, "Maggie was such a dedicated woman of faith, and she gave fully of herself to anyone who asked. Maggie never turned anyone away who was in need, even when she barely had enough for herself. Maggie not only talked the talk, but she also walked the walk, and that alone inspired anyone who crossed paths with her. God really blessed us with Maggie's life and I personally will forever be grateful for that."

Pastor Norton then closed with prayer. The first people to come up to Tom, after it was over, were a man and his wife.

The Man introduced himself and his wife, "I'm Herman, and this is my wife Bernice. We have never met you, but your mother was there when we were having trouble with our son Maurice."

Bernice added, "She took him under her wing, explained God's love to him, and he received salvation. Five months later he died in a horrible car accident, and your mother was there for us through that time of grief."

Herman said, "My son Maurice is with her in Heaven now because she was loving enough to spend time with him."

Bernice commented, "And if Miss Maggie hadn't been there to guide us through the grieving process, I don't know what would have happened."

Tom hugged them and replied, "Thank you for sharing that with me."

Next in line was a young woman with a teenage girl.

She said, "My name is Sherry, and this is my daughter Katie. Miss Maggie was the Church Grandma, when I met her. I was pregnant at sixteen.

Your mother persuaded me, and my parents, to keep my baby. I am truly grateful for that."

She hugged Tom and left.

A man approached Tom with tears in his eyes.

He said, "Miss Maggie and her church came to the prison weekly for a visit with inmates, and I was one of those inmates."

The man continued, "She told me how much God loved me, and brought me freshly baked cookies."

He went on to say, "When I was released, I changed my life. I went into a prison ministry because Miss Maggie convinced me of God's love through her actions."

A handsome man in a nice suit approached Tom.

He said, "I was homeless, and drunk, but when I knocked on Mrs. Anderson's door, she took me in. Your mother fed me, clothed me, and helped me get sober."

The man went on, "She made sure to get me involved in her church, and a member offered to let me live in his rent house for free. That man helped me get a job, and I worked my way up the corporate ladder to success, but if your mother had turned me away that day, I wouldn't be here now."

A woman dressed in jeans and a tee-shirt walked up to Tom.

She said, "This is embarrassing, but Miss

Maggie gave me a job cleaning her house, and one day she left out a necklace with a beautiful cross pendant. Before I could think about it, I grabbed it, and took off.

Now looking down, the woman in jeans continued, "She had been so nice to even give me a job. I felt bad, and brought it back. Instead of being mad and reporting me, she told me to keep it. Miss Maggie also told me that every time I looked at it to remember what Christ did for me."

In tears the woman went on to say, "I never stole anything ever again. It wasn't until later that I found out that this necklace was a Christmas present from the son who died. By then, Miss Maggie had already moved away, so I want to give it to you."

She presented the necklace to Tom, and whispered, "She showed me more grace than I deserved."

There were many more people who approached Tom with stories of how his mother was an inspiration to their lives. Tom was so proud of his mother. After Maggie's casket was lowered into her final resting place, Tom and Julie said goodbye to their mother for the last time.

Julie went to the car, and Tom stayed behind to look at Charlie's grave marker.

Tom said, "Well my work is finished with mom because I know she's with you now. I'll see you all in Heaven later. Goodbye little Brother."

Feeling like he had gotten some closure, Tom got in his car, and they drove back to Berryville, Arkansas.

11

WELCOME HOME

Maggie's funeral may have concluded the end of her life on earth, but this is only where the rest of Maggie's journey began. When Maggie closed her eyes in physical death, she was encompassed by a bright and warm light. That light proceeded from the angel that carried her to heaven.

Upon arrival the angel said, "Maggie, we are home."

Maggie stood directly in front of a massive gate made of pearl. This was the grand entrance of Heaven. The wall surrounding paradise was larger than the Great Wall of China. The Angel of God knocked on this pearly gate. As it opened, she was greeted by a great big black man wearing a white choir robe.

With a big smile on his face, he stuck out his

hand.

In a deep robust voice said, “Hello, I’m Maurice, and I will be giving you the grand tour of Heaven today!”

Maggie noticed that his warm, and friendly almond-shaped eyes twinkled with excitement. His personality was so jolly in nature that it made her feel right at home. When she lifted her hand to shake his, he gave Maggie a big hug instead.

Maggie couldn’t help but let out a laugh as she said, “Maurice, I think I really like you!”

And immediately Maggie recognized him as Herman and Bernice’s son.

She said, “I know you! You’re the little boy who grabbed my heart!”

Maurice commented, “It’s really good to see you again, thank you for introducing me to Christ.”

Maggie replied, “It was my pleasure.”

Maurice pointed out that the streets under their feet were golden. Maurice introduced Maggie to everyone who passed, as their most recent permanent resident. Maggie was really impressed with the beauty of heaven, but she had to know when she’d see Jesus and the rest of her family.

However, before she could say the first word of that sentence she was interrupted.

Maurice said, “Don’t you worry Miss Maggie you’ll see them soon, they are busy preparing for your banquet feast!”

Maggie looked at Maurice stunned as she asked, "For me?"

With a big smile he replied, "O yes my dear, all for you!"

Maggie commented, "This looks like another world all together."

Maurice grinned as he replied, "It is."

After a while, Maggie noticed the absence of any negative emotions, like sadness, anger, fear, or shame. They continued to travel further into Heaven, as the golden streets led them. The size and complexity of this place seemed amazing. Every building or structure towered far above her head. Maggie could see for miles ahead, to all of the streets, mansions, and people who she hadn't passed yet. As Maggie got closer to her destination, their guiding light got brighter, and warmer.

She thought, "We must be closing in on the sun."

Maurice approached a large wooden door.

He asked, "Maggie, are you ready to meet our Lord?"

Trying to contain her excitement Maggie responded, "Yes I'm ready"

Maurice opened the wooden door, and Maggie walked in. To her amazement there stood Jesus. Maggie fell at his feet, and began kissing them.

Jesus lifted her up and said, "Well done, my good and faithful servant. Welcome home Maggie

Ann!"

Jesus motioned for Maggie to sit at the table between Charlie and John. On the other side, sat her mother and father, who were bright eyed and smiling. Next, Maurice walked in leading the rest of the choir.

They sang, "Holy, Holy, Holy is our Lord God Almighty!"

The song was sung, and everyone in the banquet room fell to their knees to worship Jesus. Afterward Jesus invited all to the table to eat. Food was displayed on the table with gourmet style, and the room was filled with a glorious aroma. A wide variety of fruit, vegetable, meat entree, dessert, casserole, fish, and bread were arranged by food group.

Charlie said, "Hey mom, I caught those fish, and dad cooked them."

Maggie's mother said, "I made green bean casserole the way you like it."

Her father spoke up and said, "Yes and I grew the green beans in my garden."

Jesus said, "And your grandmother's famous lemon icebox pie is delicious!"

Jesus looked at her with such love in His eyes. The way Jesus looked at Maggie was so special. He knew everything about her, yet He still loved her. Maggie always thought that when she got to Heaven, she would spend all of her time with John and Charlie. But now, as she looked into the eyes of her Savior, Maggie realized that the person she wanted to spend all of her time with was Jesus! In fact, Maggie didn't want to leave His gaze.

After the feast was over, Charlie walked up to Jesus.

Charlie asked, "Do you want to go fishing with me later?"

Jesus responded, "Absolutely, I'll meet you at the pier, after you show your mom her new mansion!"

John and the rest of Maggie's family told her that they'd catch up with her later. Charlie locked arms with his mother and guided her out.

He said, "You are in for a surprise!"

His eyes beamed with pure joy. Maggie had so many questions for Charlie. For a long time Maggie had dreamed of what she'd say to Charlie, once she got to Heaven.

She asked, "So, what do you do all day?"

Charlie said, "Well I like to fish with Jesus, even though he always catches the biggest fish!"

He went on to say, "I walk around a lot to visit with everyone. There are so many people here that I still haven't talked to yet!"

Maggie said, "Well I had no idea that I would eat in Heaven."

Charlie replied, "We eat all the time here!"

He added, "We even have a welcome home celebration for all new arrivals."

Maggie was astonished, because it seemed like all these people in Heaven meant something to her.

Even though, Maggie had not known these people on earth, she still felt a connection.

Charlie remarked, "Yeah, it's a little overwhelming when you first arrive, it was for me too."

Charlie asked, "Hey do you want to take a short cut?"

Maggie responded, "Sure why not?"

She followed him off the golden street onto what was very much like grass, but much softer and thicker. Maggie realized that she was barefooted when she felt the grass between her toes. She could have laid down in that grass and taken a nap, but they continued on instead. They were walking up on a river with a bridge going over, when Maggie caught a glimpse of her own reflection. What Maggie saw surprised her, but in a good way because she could see that her gray hair was back to its natural red color. Maggie knew, by the beauty of her complection, that she had dropped more than a few years since getting to Heaven.

Charlie said, "Mama, you looked just like I remember."

She smiled and kissed him on the forehead, then they set off to cross the bridge.

Maggie had to stop, and close her eyes just to process it all. She took a deep breath. Maggie smelled a familiar fragrance, gardenias, roses, and every flower all at once. When Maggie opened her eyes, she saw parts of a dandelion flower being carried by a gentle breeze.

She asked Charlie, "Does this place ever stop unfolding into greater glory?"

He responded, "As long as I have been here, I have yet to see the same landscape twice. Every day I am wowed by God's creation!"

They reached the top of the bridge, which reminded Maggie of the accident that killed Charlie.

Maggie looked over the side as she asked, "Were you scared when you died?"

Charlie replied, "I was not alone that night. As soon as the truck left the bridge, there was an angel that stayed with me until it was time to cross over into Heaven."

Charlie grabbed his mom's hand, and guided her back to the streets of gold.

He said, "Come on Mom, there is so much more to see."

Maggie couldn't imagine there being much more than she'd already seen. This day, so far, was the best day of her whole existence.

Out of curiosity Maggie asked, "Do you suppose that the divine dreams we have, while on earth, serve a purpose to comfort us?"

Charlie replied, "Yes. Before I died physically, I had two dreams from God to prepare me for what was coming. In those dreams, Jesus reassured me that He would take care of Tom, you and Dad."

Maggie said, "Speaking of Tom, he became a priest, and took care of me to the very end."

Charlie chuckled as he responded, "Yes it's amazing how a near death experience can change a person's path."

When they reached a cross road, Charlie said, "Let's take the scenic route this time."

Maggie laughed and responded, "Which way is more scenic?"

Charlie laughed too and replied, "Well I guess they all are!"

They decided to take a detour, and turned right. Maggie smiled when they passed a field full of children playing hide-in-seek with Jesus.

Charlie dug around in the pocket of his white robe, and pulled out a handful of skittles.

Grinning Charlie asked, "Hey do you want to taste the rainbow?"

After laughing hysterically, Maggie finally caught her breath.

She asked, "Heaven has skittles?"

Charlie replied, "Heaven has anything you could ever imagine."

Maggie asked, "How does that work?"

He answered, "Well you just speak it into existence, and whatever you speak of just appears. Try it, just visualize something, and say the word."

So Maggie thought of a double rainbow raining skittles on Charlie. As soon as Maggie spoke it out loud, Charlie was pelted with skittles.

Charlie said, "Purple umbrellas!"

An umbrella sheltered him, and they both giggled.

Charlie said, "I have an idea, we will fly to my mansion!"

He closed his eyes and said, "Blueberry!"

Just like that, a blue stallion with huge white angel wings appeared. Maggie was impressed.

She asked, "Does this flying horse belong to you?"

Charlie responded, "Well, technically he belongs to God, but God let me name him and take care of him. His name is Blueberry."

Maggie chuckled and said, "For obvious reasons."

They mounted Blueberry, and in seconds were airborne. Maggie felt as free as a bird. In no time, they had reached Charlie's mansion. Maggie starred in awe, while viewing the most massive castle she'd ever seen.

Charlie dismounted and helped Maggie down.

He commented, "This baby has ten levels!"

She followed Charlie, as they crossed over the mote by way of a wooden draw bridge.

He asked, "What's a castle without a mote?"

Maggie looked over the bridge to see ten big alligators swimming around. Reaching its entrance was some challenge, but they did it. Just inside

Maggie could see a beautiful crystal chandelier hanging over a large staircase lined with teal color carpet, and white banisters.

Mother and son made their way up to the second floor.

Charlie said, "Just to let you know, there is no night in Heaven, so if you like to look at a night sky as much as I do, you'll have to come over to my mansion because I have a special room."

They walked down a hallway to a huge black door with the words written, "NIGHT". Charlie opened that door, and Maggie stepped in to see a night sky indeed. She could see stars of all sizes, some were still, while others were shooting stars. Charlie turned on a dimmer switch, and a full moon appeared, then he adjusted the switch to a half moon.

On the third floor, Maggie could hear Mozart playing. Everywhere she looked was a cultivated tree of some sort displaying a variety of fruit.

Maggie noted, "Wow you have your very own Garden of Eden!"

Charlie's forth floor exhibited an unusual environment. More like a jungle. It smelled of wild animal, or perhaps an odor similar to that of a rainforest. Maggie could hear monkeys screaming, a lion's roaring, and birds singing. That floor even felt a little more humid than the others did.

Niagra Falls was his theme for floor five, and Maggie was mystified at it's sound. She heard exactly what she'd expected raging waters to sound like. Floor six was a gourmet kitchen filled with a scent of freshly baked bread. Floor seven was filled with canvas' for painting. Some were blank, but some were completed artwork, and ready to be framed.

The eighth floor showcased instruments of every kind, from a reeded clarinet to a piano. Maggie spotted a harp sitting next to Charlie's guitar. All the walls of floor nine were windows from floor to ceiling. Multiple lounge chairs lined the walls for bird watching, people watching or even angel watching.

Finally they reached the tenth floor, and Maggie saw that it had no ceiling. Maggie could see so many white puffy clouds above. In the room's center was a large banquet style table.

Charlie said, "That table is for when I host dinner at my mansion."

Maggie stepped closer to the edge. Next door, she could see a mansion that was constructed completely out of stained glass. The stained glass exhibited colors she had never seen before.

She asked, "Who lives there?"

Charlie replied, "You do!"

Maggie jumped up and down with excitement.

She asked, "Well when can we go see it?"

Charlie answered, "Let's go right now!"

They scurried down ten flights of stairs, crossed the draw bridge, and ran next door. In shock, Maggie stood still, and gawked at this beautiful mansion that belonged to her. She noticed how gorgeous rose bushes skirted the entire glass house. Maggie walked down the pebble sidewalk lined with magnolia trees, which led to her front door. A diverse array of butterfly's swirled around Maggie's head, and humming birds fluttered their wings as if to say, "welcome home"!

Charlie looked at his mother, and said, "Well I have a fishing date with Jesus, so this is where I let you off, but I'll see you later."

Maggie continued on. Before she could turn the door knob, the door swung open. In the doorway of Maggie's Mansion stood John with a big smile.

John grabbed hold of Maggie, and squeezed her tightly.

John said, "Welcome to your Heavenly home!"

Maggie felt like she was in an elaborate Tiffany lamp. Maggie's home had a warm cozy atmosphere, and was filled with colorful rays of light. Maggie's mansion was completely illuminated by multicolored streams of light. Both, to Maggie's left and right were two separate stairs cases that led up to the second level. John held Maggie's hand, and led her upstairs. She immediately noticed the sound of waves crashing on the sea shore, and the cawing of seagulls. Maggie could even smell salt in the air, along with a hint of seaweed. Suddenly her toes were buried in warm white sand. It felt like eighty degrees with a warm breeze. The wind caused her white robe to sway. Hand in hand Maggie and John waded into the ocean.

Maggie said, "When you died, I didn't think I would make it, but God showed me that if I would lean on Him, He could still use me."

John replied, "The night before I died, Jesus came to me in a dream. He told me not to worry about leaving you behind because He took special care in watching over widows. Jesus also told me that you would lead a lot of people to him."

Maggie asked, "Who are we that God cares so much for us?"

John smiled and said, "We are His beloved children!"

They enjoyed a moment of peaceful silence. Maggie closed her eyes as she basked in the warmth of sun light.

John said, "Well I can show you the rest of your mansion, but it's basically a blank canvas awaiting your own personal touch."

Maggie responded, "I want to see what your mansion looks like."

John's eyes twinkled, and he grabbed her hand.

He said, "Okay, it's right next door!"

Maggie followed John back to the golden street, then turned right. They walked some ways, and stopped in front of a black rod iron fence. At the top of the rod iron fence was written "John's Ranch". John proudly showed Maggie his variety of cattle, sheep, and horses. His animal's lived peacefully together on all sides of his ranch style mansion. John's mansion sat atop a tall hill. The path that led there was a dirt road, very rugged, and manly.

Maggie laughed as she commented, "So not only does our spirit come to heaven, but our personality comes too."

John said, "Yeah, I can't wait to see how your personality shines through your mansion!"

John's interior was definitely Southwestern minus a mounted buck and bear skinned rugs. Maggie walked through his solid oak double doors, and sat on a big soft leather sofa.

John came in and asked Maggie, "Did you ever find Mary, the baby you had at seventeen?"

Maggie smiled and replied, "I thought you'd never ask."

She went on to say, "Her name is Julie, and she looks just like me!"

John said, "Tell me more."

Maggie said, "She's sweet, a nurse, who by the way, took care of me, when I was at Grandview Nursing Home, before realizing that I was her birth mother."

She continued, "I must give God credit for that one for sure!"

Maggie could tell John was curious about Tom

so she said, "And Tom went on to become a priest for the Catholic Church!"

John was surprised and said, "Wow I never saw that coming!"

Maggie responded, "Me either, that must have been a divine interference!"

They both laughed.

12

MAGGIE'S VISIT WITH GOD

John told Maggie how much Maurice really admired her. Maggie smiled in thinking that Maurice thought so highly of her.

Maggie suggested, "Show me some more of Heaven."

John said, "Okay, follow me."

They walked out through the massive double door of John's mansion, and down the pathway to the golden street. Maggie was met by a woman who hugged her, and kissed her cheek. When the woman stepped back, Maggie recognized that it was Grandma Harrison.

Maggie said, "Oh I'm so glad to see you! Priscilla asked me to find you when I got to heaven, and tell you, that she will be home soon and loves you!"

Grandma Harrison smiled and said, "Thank you, sweet-pea!"

John and Maggie continued their walk. She noticed that a few mansions that were not complete.

Maggie asked, "Why are those mansions unfinished?"

John answered, "Oh, those are for the people who haven't died physically yet, but with every good deed they do in the name of Christ, more progress is made on their mansion."

John remarked, "Remember in scripture Jesus saying, not to store up for your selves treasures on earth, where moth and rust destroy, and thieves break in and steal. Instead, lay up for yourselves treasures in Heaven, where neither moth nor rust destroys, and where thieves do not break in and steal. For where your treasure is, there, your heart will be also."

John went on to say, "You see, admission into this paradise is free, when you believe in your heart, and confess with your mouth Jesus Christ as Lord. However, your reward, in this paradise, comes while living in the physical realm because of your love for Christ, you do things for the least important people, the outcasts, and less fortunate who cannot return the favor."

Maggie responded, "Wow, I never thought of it like that."

John said, "Hey, I know a really good dinner

that serves some of the best apple pie!"

When they got to the dinner, John opened the door for Maggie, and that's when she saw Sister Agnus!

Sister Agnus smiled and said, "I heard we had new arrival, today."

Maggie walked up to Sister Agnus, and asked, "Is this your dinner?"

Sister Agnus answered, "Yes. I have always dreamed of owning, and operating my own dinner!"

Maggie said, "I had an opportunity to meet my daughter, and she still had the quilt that I asked you to send with her. Thank you for doing that!"

Sister Agnus said, "I'm just glad I could help."

Sister Agnus set a plate of hot steaming apple pie, with a scoop of vanilla ice cream on top, in front of Maggie.

Sister Agnus said, "Eat up!"

Sister Agnus also set a plate of dessert in front of John.

She said, "Don't worry, there is more where that came from."

After Maggie and John finished their pie, she thanked Agnus, and they left the dinner. John saw that Maggie was looking up to find the source of heaven's light.

John stated, "If your looking for a sun or light bulb, you won't find it. The Glory of God, His Holy Spirit, is heaven's source of light, so the sun and moon are not needed."

Maggie replied, "You know that makes perfect sense. While still alive physically, I noticed some people seemed a little bit brighter than other folks. Come to find out, they were followers of Christ. That glow must have come from having the Holy Spirit dwell inside them. Now that you mention it, I do remember reading in scripture that there would be no need of a sun."

Maggie was deep in thought when John asked, "So is Heaven any different from the way you imagined it would be?"

Maggie replied, "Are you kidding? I'm so amazed that I really never gave it much thought. I figured we would have a harp, but probably just float around on a cloud, for eternity!"

John laughed and responded, "I think a lot of us don't really know what to expect when we get to Heaven. It's kinda like, anything a person has ever desired to do or be, becomes a possibility here."

John went on, "There's a man here that was a preacher in the physical world, so what do you think he does up here?"

Maggie guessed, "Does he preach?"

John said, "That's right. Not that Heaven needs a preacher to teach about Christ or God, but that's what he loves to do."

John continued, "God encourages us to do what moves us, however, the purpose of everything we do in heaven is to serve each other, and to serve God our Father and Jesus His Son."

John paused for a moment then proceeded, "For instance, you know I like to work with my hands building furniture and houses. Supply and demand is not an issue in Heaven. Therefore, I can build things for my own enjoyment."

Maggie said, "Yes I know you like to build, and that reminds me. The log-cabin you built me, burned down to the ground."

John replied, "Don't worry about that because I built a replica here in heaven for you!"

Then he said, "Isn't it amazing how our physical life was such a fleeting moment, and now is just a distant memory?"

Maggie smiled and said, "Yes, it is amazing, but when are you going to show me the replica?"

John said, "Okay, but I must admit I didn't build it on my own. I had the help of a master carpenter!"

Maggie exclaimed, "Jesus helped you build my gift?"

John replied, "Yes He did!"

Maggie realized that there were not any angels beyond the pearly gate.

Maggie asked, "Where are all the angels at?"

John said, "God's Angel's are always busy bringing messages to people on earth, and looking after God's creation. Sometimes Angel's are fighting

Satan and his demons' on behalf of God's children. God's Angel's are also busy transporting souls to Heaven. So usually they are only present for Worship. Even then, they are responsible for leading the worship service."

Maggie was stunned and said, "Wow, they're always busy. His Angel's are magnificent creatures!"

Maggie stopped walking, and turned to look at John.

She asked, "So when do I get to talk to the Man in charge?"

John asked, "You mean God our Creator?"

Maggie replied, "Yes, God my Father."

John responded, "We are on our way there now, He's waiting for you."

Maggie could hardly contain her excitement, as she thought of all the questions she had for God to answer. The scenery around Maggie was beginning to change, and becoming more mountainous. Maggie didn't ask any more questions. Instead, she followed John up a trail to the mountaintop, where a log cabin sat.

John said, "Here is your gift, and God is inside waiting for you."

John stayed behind, as Maggie walked the rest of the way alone.

She walked through the front door and asked, "God, are you in here?"

From the back porch, she could hear a man's

voice say, "I'm back here Maggie Ann."

Maggie walked through her cabin, and out the back door. She could see an average size, middle age man standing with his arms' wide open. As soon as Maggie stepped out on the back porch, God embraced her. Maggie buried her face in His chest, and He stroked her hair.

She thought, "How could I feel so comfortable in Almighty God's embrace?"

God, knowing Maggie's thoughts, replied, "Maggie, you feel comfortable because I'm your creator, and I put eternity in your heart!"

Maggie was speechless. God sat down on a porch swing, and patted the seat beside Him for her to sit. Maggie sat down, and they watched the rain in silence for a while.

Maggie broke the silence first.

She stated, "I didn't think it would rain in Heaven."

God smiled and replied, "Well technically we don't need rain in paradise."

God continued, "But I know how much you enjoy it."

Maggie responded, "All this seems a bit much for one person."

God said, "Maggie, my love for you is limitless and certainly has no boundary!"

Maggie looked into God's eyes, searching for this love He spoke of, but after only a few moments she had to look away because God's loving gaze was so intense.

Sitting on a porch swing with God, and enjoying a rain storm together was never what Maggie expected. She had always envisioned God sitting on His throne, while the rest of Heaven served Him. So, this experience was a pleasant surprise. Maggie could have sat the rest of eternity there with God swinging in silence. Maggie was satisfied in God's presence, but there were still questions she wanted to ask Him.

God must have known because He said, "It's okay, ask me."

Maggie skirting the issue said, "You know what my questions are. Why do I have to ask them in order for you to answer them?"

God responded, "You would miss out on asking. Besides, I like hearing what you say even if I already know what you will ask."

Maggie took a deep breath and asked, "Why was my life on earth so hard?"

She continued, "I mean, I realize that my first loss was a result of my own sin of fornication, but I can't understand what the reason or purpose was for losing my fourteen-year-old son to death, and my other son to sorrow."

God put His arm around Maggie.

He said, "Tell me why you enjoy a rain storm."

Maggie responded, "Well I think that there is

something refreshing about rain. Without it, flowers or trees wouldn't grow."

God said, "Okay, now tell me what you do not enjoy about rain."

Maggie replied, "Well, rain sometimes stops outside activity for humans, and birds are grounded by rain."

God asked, "So even though humans and birds have brief undesired moments of hardship because of the rain, would you say that it's still necessary?"

Maggie said, "Well of course! If it never rained, then the birds would have no tree's to build their nests. For humans, rain is needed for drinking water and to water crops."

God said, "Ah, so you think the pro's outweigh the con's. The risk is worth the benefit, right?"

Maggie nodded yes.

God continued, "However, unlike the rain I do not send suffering, and I certainly do not enjoy watching anyone suffer, but I do rejoice when out of that suffering I can produce something good. Perhaps, I can produce some fruit of the Spirit that I like to call Godly Character."

God said, "Suffering and death were not in my original plan, but sin and death entered into the world as a result of Adam's disobedience."

He continued, "So like any good father, you work with what you have, and what you have is a broken world where good people suffer."

He said, "So I sent, My only Son, Jesus to pay the wages of sin, with His death. Jesus came to conquer death with His bodily resurrection. Then, to ascend to heaven, and sit at my right hand. Consequently, the actions of Jesus made a way for Me to be with mankind again through My Holy Spirit. Finally, the death and resurrection of Christ paved the way to eternity for a believer's at their physical death."

God commented, "So you asked me why your life was so hard. And I say that, Jesus, the Holy Spirit, and I work with what We have. Our goal is not to change the outward situation, but to change the inward person. In other words, we change your reaction to outside influence. You're meant to learn how to overcome struggles from the inside. "

He said, "We bring something good out of everything that hurts you."

God said, "Nothing that happens to my creation ever goes to waste."

Maggie kept quiet, and just listened as God continued.

He said, "You mentioned all of your heartache, but let me tell you of all the fruit that your heartache produced."

God squeezed Maggie's shoulder, and smiled.

He said, "So that you don't get the big head, I'll only mention a few!"

Maggie giggled, and said, "Go on!"

God responded, "Before you died physically your daughter, Julie, acknowledged the power of prayer."

Maggie asked, "What do you mean?"

God responded, "Julie had been praying to find her birth mother since she was five-years-old."

Maggie asked, "Why did you wait so long to answer her prayer?"

God answered, "Maggie, you were the reason I waited so long to answer Julie's prayer. You weren't ready to face reality until the end of your life."

He said, "At Grandview Nursing Home you prayed for Priscilla, and I sent Tom to minister to her through you."

God stated, "Charlie's death was hard on you, but it was harder on Tom, yet it caused him to turn to Me for comfort and strength."

He continued, "John's death, taught you to completely depend on Me."

Without hesitation God went on, "At your grave side service in Texas, Tom was approached by Sherry. Sherry told Tom that you were responsible for talking her into keeping Kiley, the daughter born out of wedlock. Kiley went on to talk to young girls about the importance of abstinence."

He said, "Timothy was once a homeless drunk, but you introduced him to my Son Jesus, and showed him love and kindness."

He went on, "Oh yes and Maurice was a double whammy!"

God said, "Maurice reminded you of Tom's stubbornness, and you were determined to reach him. You took him under your wing. When he died, you helped his parents get though their grieving process. Because you lost Charlie, you knew exactly what they were going through."

He stated, "Sister Agnus was blessed for giving that quilt to the parents that adopted Julie. The parents who adopted Julie had been asking Me, for ten years, to give them a child. So, you blessed them too."

He commented, "What about young Meredith, who you hired to clean your house. She stole the necklace Charlie gave you, but you showed her grace and mercy, which changed her life."

God paused for a moment to allow all that he said to sink into Maggie's mind.

Then He preceded, "Are you beginning to see the bigger picture?"

Maggie answered, ":Yes, it is much more clear."

God said, "Now knowing all this, and all the people that you touched, would you change anything that you suffered?"

Maggie looked at God, and hugged his neck.

She said, "No, I wouldn't change a thing!"

Maggie realized that there was a single tear rolling down her cheek, but God wiped it away.

He said, "You know since I have wiped away all your tears, there is no more crying in heaven."

They both smiled, and God stood up.

He said, "Come on there is still so much more to see."

Maggie got up and followed God through her cabin, down a mountain and to the golden street.

When they reached the golden street God smiled at Maggie and commented, "Guess where the wizard of oz got his yellow brick road."

Maggie looked around, and laughed.

She said, "God I don't think we're in Texas any longer!"

God laughed with a big belly laugh and they walked arm in arm singing, "We're off to see the Savior, the wonderful Savior of all."

13

GONE BOATING

Maggie and God were walking along, just enjoying each others company, when a lady approached them. In her arms, she cradled a colorful bouquet of flowers.

God said, "Rita, this is Maggie."

Maggie stuck out her hand, but Rita hugged her instead.

Rita said, "Maggie honey, I'm a hugger!"

Maggie asked, "Did you grow those flowers?"

Rita replied, "Technically God grew them, but I did plant them. I hope you like them because they're for you!"

With a smile Rita handed Maggie the beautiful bouquet of fresh-cut flowers.

Rita said, "Welcome to heaven, we're so glad to have you!"

Rita hugged God, and kissed His cheek.

Rita said, "Well I better get back to my garden, see you later."

Maggie looked at God and thought, "He is so much more approachable than I ever imagined."

A little farther ahead Maggie could see a crowd gathered around a large oak tree. Maggie could not see Jesus, because of the crowd, but she knew it was His voice from within the center of that crowd.

God said, "Jesus makes me so proud!"

Maggie watched as God looked at Jesus with such affection.

She thought, "That's something special, to have the Creator of all life say that you make Him proud."

God looked at Maggie and said, "I'm proud of you too, Maggie."

They walked closer to get a better look. Maggie could see Jesus teaching as He sat on the grass under a shady oak tree. God sat amongst the crowd. Maggie sat next to God, and listened as Jesus taught.

Jesus said, "Blessed were the poor in spirit, for theirs is now the kingdom of heaven. Blessed are those who mourned, for they have now been comforted. Blessed are the meek, for they have now inherited the earth. Blessed are those who hungered and thirsted for righteousness, for now they are filled. Blessed were the merciful, for they have obtained mercy. Blessed are the pure in heart, for they now see

God's face. Blessed are the peacemakers, for they are called the son's of God. Blessed are those who were persecuted for righteousness' sake, for theirs is the kingdom of heaven."

God looked over at Maggie and said, "For whoever desires to save his life will lose it, but whoever loses his life for My Son's sake will find it."

Maggie responded, "I always wondered what Jesus meant when he talked about how a person is blessed if they were sad, or poor in spirit, but if the purpose some how served to reach people for Christ well then I understand."

Maggie surprised herself. God just smiled, and winked at her. The crowd dispersed, as Jesus finished speaking. He made his way down to greet Maggie and God.

As He embraced His Father, Jesus said, "Abba!"

God stated, "You teach that principle so well!"

Maggie just watched, in amazement, how they interacted together.

Finally, Jesus turned to Maggie and asked, "Would you like to go out on the boat with me?"

Maggie replied, "Yes Lord, I would love to."

God said, "You two have fun, I'll catch you later."

He then walked away pretending to cast and pull in an invisible net, laughing.

Jesus smiled saying, "He's such a cut up."

They walked down a path along the lake, and climbed into a small boat. Jesus paddled toward the center of the lake, then stopped rowing. Maggie watched as Jesus pulled in the ore's and reclined. He propped both feet up, and interlocked His hands behind His head.

Jesus closed His eyes, and asked, "What are you thinking about?"

Maggie's heart burned within her. She recalled all the times that she had only seen a glimpse of God's Glory, but now was experiencing the full weight of it.

Maggie asked, "Were you always there with me?"

Without moving Jesus said, "Every moment of you life, good and bad."

Maggie smiled, then leaned back to relax.

She asked, "Why?"

Jesus answered, "We created mankind for our good pleasure, not for mankind to be alone."

Then stated, "When Adam and Eve sinned in the Garden, Our plan was momentarily interrupted. So I, The Father and His Holy Spirit made a decision that would set Our original plan back on track. The plan involved Our sacrifice to redeem mankind once and for all. To redeem all those who would believe in Me."

Maggie paused for a moment then asked, "So did I fulfil my purpose on earth?"

Jesus replied, "Well it depends on what you

think your purpose was."

Maggie sat up with a puzzled look on her face.

She asked, "Huh?"

Jesus smiled, sat up and met Maggie's gaze.

He said, "Let me explain."

Maggie said, "Yes please do."

Jesus stated, "Most people think of their lives on earth as a straight line, sort of like a time line with a beginning and an end. However, the way people really live out their earthly lives is much like a circle. Ending where they began because human life makes a full circle prior to physical death."

Jesus went on, "For you Maggie, in death you faced everything that life left undone. You made peace with how you had lived, and left life the way you entered, with nothing but love."

He continued, "On your death bed, you discovered that what matters the most, exists beyond what is seen."

Maggie said, "Okay, well then what was my purpose?"

Jesus answered, "Your purpose was to love God, and be loved by Him. The way a believer lives their life is the living testimony of God's love."

Maggie still not sure asked, "So why the roller coaster life?"

Jesus responded, "When Tom was a toddler learning how to walk, did he ever fall?"

Maggie answered, "Yes."

He asked, "Well when Tom fell, did you run to pick him up, and carry him the rest of his life?"

Maggie said, "No, sometimes I pretended not to see him, so he'd get up and try again."

Jesus said, "So, was your reason because you didn't care or didn't love him?"

Maggie said, "Of course not, it was because of my love for him that I didn't run and pick him up every time he fell."

Jesus kept silent, and Maggie thought for a moment.

She said, "I think I understand now. I did not cause Tom to fall, but I allowed the fall. It was not life threatening, and that was the only way he'd learn how to walk, by learning from his mistakes!"

Jesus stood up, and reached for Maggie's hand to help her up.

She said, "Let me guess! We are going to walk back to shore!"

Jesus laughed out loud and said, "Well walking on the water has already been done so many times. I thought you and I might race instead!"

Maggie was ready for an adventure.

She said, "You know me too well!"

Then she said, "On your mark, get set, go!"

Maggie and Jesus both grabbed the bottom of their robes, hopped out of the boat, and took off. Jesus reached the shore first, threw up his hands, and did a victory dance. Maggie laughed as she finally caught up to him, then imitated the dance.

Jesus turned to Maggie with a more serous look on His face.

He said, "Avery will be here soon, and we have some work to do. I'll prepare his feast in the banquet room, while you gather up the family. I'll meet you there."

Maggie excitedly relied, "Okay!"

Maggie hurried off to inform her mother, father, and the rest of the welcoming home committee. On the way to her mother's mansion Maggie ran into God.

God said, "I was looking for you. Tom asked me to give you a message in his prayers today. He wanted me to tell you that he loves you, and is thinking of you."

Maggie smiled and asked, "I'm not sure how this works, but can you tell him I love him too, and that I am happy here?"

God said, "Maggie, I am God, and I can do anything, so I'll send him a dream of you okay."

Maggie responded, "Thanks, you're the greatest!"

Then she hugged him and said, "I'm on my way to mom's mansion to tell her about Avery."

God said, "I know."

Maggie smiled and continued on. When Maggie arrived, her mother and father were sitting on the porch swing together in front.

Maggie said, "Avery's on his way, and Jesus told me to gather you all for his feast."

Her mother and father were overjoyed, and jumped up to get the rest of their family together.

Maggie's father said, "Before we head out to meet Avery, I have something to give you."

He walked next door to his mansion, grabbed a bag and brought it back.

Maggie asked, "What's this?"

Her father said, "Look and see."

Maggie carefully opened the brown bag to see apples and oranges!

She looked up at her dad and said, "Thank you, daddy!"

Maggie's father said, "Some traditions just follow us to heaven!"

Maggie replied, "Thank you for being such a great father."

He continued, "Speaking of traditions, do you want to help me build some fences later?"

With a big smile Maggie answered, "Absolutely!"

She then looked at her mother and said, "Thank you for being strong for me."

Maggie's mother replied, "I did the best I could with what I knew. I'm sorry for the mistakes I made along the way."

Maggie said, "You were the best mother!"

They hugged each other. Maggie's mother

grabbed a package off the swing, and gave it to her. Maggie opened it, and found the most beautiful lap quilt she'd ever seen.

Maggie asked, "Mom, do you remember that lap quilt you made me for Christmas the year I was at St. Anthony's?"

Maggie's mother responded, "Yes, how could I forget."

Maggie said, "Well I asked Sister Agnus to give that quilt to the parents that adopted my baby. Sister Agnus did pass the quilt on, and the best part was when I met Julie, she showed it to me. Julie had kept it all those years."

Maggie's mother smiled and hugged her. Maggie's mother and father left to gather the rest of their family. So, Maggie sat on her mother's porch swing.

14

HOLY SPIRIT ENCOUNTER

While Maggie was swinging, a man approached her and asked, "Do you mind if I sit with you?"

Maggie scooted over and responded, "No, please sit."

The man said, "Isn't it beautiful here?"

Maggie replied, "Yes, more beautiful than I had ever imagined!"

Maggie noticed that there was something different about this man, but couldn't seem to put her finger on it.

She thought, "There is an intensity about him that I recognize."

About that time, the man sitting next to Maggie made eye contact, and she felt her whole body tremble. Then he placed his hand on Maggie's arm, and she felt a tremendous amount of power surging through her entire being. Maggie realized immediately that the man sitting beside her was The Holy Spirit. As a result of His touch, Maggie was filled with wisdom, understanding, and knowledge of all things.

Maggie said, "John told me that you were heavens light source."

The Holy Spirit smiled and replied, "Surely you didn't expect Me to look like a light bulb huh?"

Maggie's eyes widened, as she shrugged her shoulders.

The Holy Spirit responded, "Well the glory of God is heaven's light source. I am part of that, but I also function in other way's too."

Maggie commented, "Oh, well that may explain why I always had a hard time seeing you in a bodily form."

The Holy Spirit responded, "I can take any form necessary to accomplish any task. For example, when John baptized Jesus, My decent on Jesus was in the form of a dove. When the apostle's were baptized with My Spirit, I was the tongue of flames. When Moses led the Israelites out of Egypt, I went before them by day in a pillar of a cloud, and by night in a pillar of fire to give them light."

Maggie asked, "So this man I see before me, who sits with me on this swing, is not your true form?"

The Holy Spirit answered, "Oh heaven's no, but in order to accomplish the task of sitting next to you on this swing, I took the form of a man."

Maggie asked, "Will I ever see You in Your true form?"

The Holy Spirit said, "Later, when all of the heavenly host's join together for worship, you will see me as I truly am."

Maggie inquired, "Well can you give me a hint?"

The Holy Spirit smiled and said, "Okay, since you persist. I am the Spirit of the Lord, the very nature of God the creator. Within me abides wisdom, insightful understanding, of what is true, right, and enduring."

He went on, "Within Me is wise counsel, meaning advice or guidance."

The Holy Spirit stated, "And lets not forget, I am full of might, meaning force or power."

He continued, "Within me is knowledge, the understanding achieved through experience."

The Holy Spirit said, "The fear of the Lord, in other word's, reverence and awe!"

Maggie in awe said, "So you're like the total package huh?"

The Holy Spirit chuckled and replied, "Yes, you could say that!"

Maggie said, "Will you tell me why Jesus had to die before You could dwell within mankind?"

The Holy Spirit responded, "It's not as complicated as you think. God is Holy, just, and righteous. God is one who always keeps His word. He warned Adam and Eve that the natural consequence of disobeying His command would bring death. Having free-will, they chose to sin.

He said, "God will always stay true to Himself, so from then on mankind had a sinful nature, and sin's consequence is death."

The Holy Spirit continued, "The price of sin had to be paid because sin cannot coexist with God's righteousness."

He stated, "So if I had dwelt in mankind after the fall, and before the death and resurrection of Jesus, mankind would have been burned up by my presence."

He went on, "As an act of grace, I waited until Christ took the full punishment of all sin to come, before I would dwell with mankind. I bring the full nature of God through the righteousness of Christ's sacrifice."

He said, "Because of Christ's sacrifice, mankind is now absolved of their sins. When God looks down on the earth, He sees the face Jesus in every believer. He smells the beautiful fragrance of His Son in all those who choose to make Christ the Lord of their lives."

The Holy Spirit commented, "By the way, the reason God commands mankind not to sin is because when they sin, it hurts them, others and God."

Maggie was suddenly filled with joy, peace,

and happiness.

She stated, "So God created mankind, gave us choice, then paid the price for our poor choices by dying to save us from the total destruction, which we brought on ourselves!"

The Holy Spirit responded, "Well, that description is definitely a good start. However, in order to have a better understanding, you must know why God chose to save mankind."

Maggie thought about it for a moment then asked, "Is it because of His love for us?"

The Holy Spirit replied, "Yes. His unconditional, unfailing, merciful, pure, and undefiled love for mankind!"

Maggie said, "Wow that's deep!"

The Holy Spirit laughed.

He commented, "Deeper than the deepest deep!"

Maggie asked, "You said those who made Jesus Lord of their lives, what does that actually mean?"

The Holy Spirit answered, "The word lord means a man with dominion, and power over others. Here is some word history: The actual as well as the symbolic importance of bread as a basic foodstuff is exhibited by the word lord. The word Lord is derived from a compound formed in very ancient times from the words hlaf, (bread) and weard, (ward, guardian) Lord, therefore literally means (guardian of the bread).

Since such a position was the dominant one in a household, lord came to denote a man of authority, and rank in society at large."

Maggie looking a little confused asked, "Could you put that in simpler terms?"

The Holy Spirit said, "Well that was how Webster's dictionary defined it!"

Maggie smiled and said, "But I want to know what the higher authority has to say about it, not the Webster Dictionary."

The Holy Spirit said, "I see your point, Jesus called himself the bread of life. He said that those who came to Him would never again hunger, and those that believed on him would never again thirst."

He went on, "So, as bread was essential to sustain life on earth, Christ is essential to obtain life eternal."

Maggie responded, "So that's what participation in communion at church was all about. The bread representing the broken body of Christ, and the wine representing the blood of Christ shed for us."

The Holy Spirit replied, "Yes the earthly practice of communion is symbolic of receiving Christ into your self. You are accepting the guardian of the bread (life) to become guardian of your life. You see everything done on earth is but a shadow of the heavenly unseen things, like a model airplane is to a life size plane, or a doll house is to a life size house."

Maggie was so amazed, but still desired to

know more.

She asked, "Okay now what about water baptism?"

The Holy Spirit answered, "In keeping with a model airplane to the life-sized ratio, water baptism is symbolic of dying with Christ. So, in getting baptized, a follower of the way (Christ) accepts God's call on their life, no matter what their calling may require."

He continued, "They die or give up their own desires and wants, to serve God with their life."

The Holy Spirit said, "It also represents being cleansed of all their sins with an attitude of repentance, which prepares the way for Me. So, water baptism is symbolic of being baptized with the Holy Spirit, but at the same time grace is imparted into the person's heart."

He went on, "As soon as Jesus received water baptism by John, I came down from heaven in the form of a dove, and stayed on Jesus. Then, I drove Him into the wilderness for forty days."

He continued, "With water baptism, also a means of grace, the believer is accepting whatever God has called them to do. The baptism of the Spirit empowers you to endure, or persevere in whatever God has called you to."

The Holy Spirit asked, "You got anything else?"

Maggie answered, "As a matter of fact I do, what about all the different denominations within

Christianity, which one had the correct answer?"

The Holy Spirit laughed, but stopped when He noticed that Maggie wasn't laughing.

He said, "Oh, you were serious about that?"

Maggie said, "They all claimed to be the ones that had it right."

The Holy Spirit replied, "Yes, you are right, but here's the thing, if you look at the human body for example, it is made up of many different parts that serves different purposes."

He said, "Take the ears, they differ from the eyes, but would the ears say to the eyes be gone, there is no need for you because you don't hear, of course not!"

He went on, "Or the feet say to the hand, because you don't balance the body, there is not any need of you!"

He said, "So Christianity is the body, and all the different denominations like Catholic, Orthodox, Baptist, Methodist, Lutheran, Presbyterian, Churches of Christ, Assembly of God, United Pentecostal, Christian Church and the Church of God, etc. are all the different body parts that serves a variety of purposes equally."

The Holy Spirit said, "And their sole purpose should be, to go out into all the earth, and spread the good news of the gospel. God wants to show the rest of mankind the love of Christ through their words and actions. As often as they feel led by Me to do so."

The Holy Spirit leaned back, kicked his feet out to cross them, and interlocked his fingers behind his head. The Holy Spirit looked over at Maggie, and grinned like he was proud of his explanation.

Maggie said, "What's your favorite way to speak to people?"

The Holy Spirit sat up straight and responded, "All ways, but mostly it's dependant on the person. Like if they are expecting to find God in an earthquake or something big, I like to speak to them in a still small voice. Or if a person expects to hear me in a still small voice, I like to speak a little more dramatic, as through a burning bush. Reenforcing the idea to expect the unexpected, you know what I mean jellybean."

Maggie said, "I understand rubber band!" They looked at each other and both laughed.

Maggie said, "One last question for now, how are you dwelling with mankind, but here with me in heaven at the same time?"

The Holy Spirit responded, "That's easy, I am God, the Holy Spirit, omnipotent meaning all powerful, and omnipresent meaning I can be everywhere at the same time."

Maggie sat there, and allowed His words to sink in.

The Holy Spirit asked, "Aren't you going to ask me about the Bible?"

He went on, "I know that you want to know if

the Bible you studied was inspired by God, or just written by a bunch of men, so ask."

Maggie replied, "Well now that you put me on the spot."

She continued, "I had faith that it was divinely inspired by God, tell me, was I right?"

The Holy Spirit responded, "Yes, I personally brought the word of God, and compelled men to write word for word, in which they were anointed for."

He explained further, "I put God's word in their heart. I was the motivation, passion, and power behind their writing. I even supplied the strength required to move their writing instrument."

Maggie said, "Heaven just keeps getting better and more interesting every moment!"

The Holy Spirit smiled and commented, "You have only scratched the surface! By the way, you had better get to the banquet room so you can greet Avery when he gets here!"

Maggie hopped up and said, "Whoa, I completely got distracted, yeah you're right I've got to get going, see you later!"

Maggie headed down the golden street, and realized she knew exactly where she was going.

She thought, "Wow, this must be one of the many perks of heaven."

Maggie arrived, and sat by John and Charlie. Suddenly, the large heavy wooden doors opened. There stood Avery, with his eyes full of tears, looking overwhelmed with joy. Maggie couldn't help herself. She just ran up to Avery, and squeezed him tight.

She said, "I'm glad you're home bubba!"

Avery sat down beside their mother and father, but still bewildered, he didn't say too much.

Maggie thought, "This is what I must have looked like when I first got here."

Addressing Avery, she said, "It takes a little while to process this, but I'll show you some of the ropes!"

Avery smiled at his sister and said, "Good, I have missed you, Maggie!"

Jesus walked up behind Avery, and touched him on his shoulder.

Jesus said, "Welcome home my friend."

Avery turned around, got up, and hugged Jesus with a manly bear hug.

Jesus laughed and said, "I have been waiting for that hug your whole life Avery!"

Avery sat back down, grabbed his mother and father's hand.

Avery said, "Mama and daddy, I have missed all of you so much!"

His mother smiled, and kissed Avery's hand. After the feast was over Maggie, locked arms with Avery.

Maggie asked, "Are you ready for a tour of Heaven?"

Avery smiled and answered, "Absolutely, let's

get started!"

They walked out of the banquet room together, and toward his mansion.

After a while Avery asked Maggie, "Aren't you curious about how Julie's doing?"

Maggie responded, "Oh yes, I just wanted your heavenly arrival to be about you and not me."

She went on to say, "But since you mentioned it, how is she coming along?"

Avery answered, "Oh Maggie, you'd be so proud of her. After you died, Julie quit her job at the nursing home. Tom helped her get connected with an organization that helps families locate children who were given up for adoption and vice versa!"

Avery stated, "Julie is very active in that organization, and she also gives talks at conferences all over the world. Her talks cover every thing regarding Alzheimer's disease. Julie even gives advice on how to deal with it from a professional, and personal aspect."

All Maggie could say was, "Praise God!"

15

THROUGH EYES OF AN ANGEL

They saw Jesus walking along a lake, and Maggie ran ahead to meet Him.

When Maggie reached Him, she asked, "Will you let me wash your feet? After reading that You washed the disciple's feet, I have always wanted to wash Your feet."

Jesus sweetly smiled and said, "Yes you may."

Jesus sat down beside the lake, and Maggie got on her knees before Him. She cupped water from the lake to pour over His feet. Maggie remembered the feeling she experienced while cleaning the altar table at her church.

Maggie said, "Wow, when I was on earth I remember feeling like I do now because it was like by washing the legs of the altar I was really washing your feet, Jesus!"

Jesus replied, "Yes, I remember that day. You felt that way because when a believer does anything on earth in My name, it's as though they are actually doing it unto Me. That really pleases The Father."

As Maggie washed Jesus' feet, she examined every inch including the scars.

Then Maggie looked into the mesmerizing eyes of her Savior.

She said, "Thank you for loving me the way that you do, but why?"

Jesus responded, "Maggie, The Father, The Holy Spirit and I created you so that We could love you with a strong love that never lets go."

Jesus continued, "A love designed to pierce your soul, and draw you closer to the heart of God."

He said, "Love that is jealous, and possessive. A love that in and of itself has the ability to set a heart ablaze with fire. A love that causes a heart to yearn for more,"

He commented, "Nothing about the way I love you, is pansy or puppy love, and certainly not cute or sissy."

Jesus went on, "Our love for you is so pure, sweet, and undefiled. It is the most concentrated form of unconditional love that exists."

He said, "Our love is the kind that makes the recipient strive to be Holy for God is Holy."

He stated, "However, the same love I speak of

is also patient, kind, and longsuffering."

Maggie noticed that as Jesus spoke about His love for her, that the light He emitted got brighter.

She said, "That is fierce!"

Then Maggie dried his feet with her robe.

She said, "Jesus, Avery told me how well Julie is doing, but I want to see for myself. Is there any way I can look down on her from Heaven?"

Jesus stood up and said, "Well lets go see what the Father has to say."

About that time Avery walked up and said, "Maggie, hurry you have got to see this!"

She and Jesus followed Avery to a patch of wooded area. He pointed to a great big lion that was walking around with animals that should have been in his belly. Just then, out of the near by brush, a little lamb ran out in front of the lion. A massive lion, king of the jungle, took notice, and charged toward the lamb.

Avery looked back at Jesus and said, "Oh my gosh! Is the lion going to eat the lamb?"

Jesus burst into a fit of laughter, while Avery focused his attention back to the scene unfolding. When the lion reached the lamb, he just licked its head. They were wrestling like you'd expect two puppies to roll around together. Avery scratched his head in confusion, as he looked at Maggie for explanation.

With a smile Maggie said, "Avery, do you

remember the passage of scripture where it says the lion will lay down with the lamb?"

He replied, "Oh yeah, now that you mention it, I do."

Avery asked, "Okay now, when do I get to see my mansion?"

Jesus responded, "All aboard, next stop is Avery's Mansion!"

Rubbing his hands together with excitement Avery shouted, "Whoopee!"

A massive tree came into view. As they got closer, Maggie realized that Avery's mansion was an enormous tree house.

Avery ran ahead of Maggie and Jesus yelling, "I'll catch you later!"

Maggie looked at Jesus, and flashed Him a smile.

She commented, "You can really tell a lot about people by their mansion huh?"

Jesus said, "That's for sure."

Maggie asked, "Do you think God will let me look down on Julie?"

Jesus said, "Well, we're fixing to find out because we're here."

Maggie looked around, and spotted God the Father. God was sitting at a potter's wheel, and molding clay.

The Father acknowledged their presence with a nod.

He said, "Maggie, come sit down."

Jesus nudged Maggie before He left.

Jesus said, "Go ahead, I'll talk more with you later."

Maggie made her way over to God, and sat down.

She asked, "Why do you like to make clay pots, when you could make other things more marvelous?"

God eyes never left the clay He was molding, while He spoke to Maggie.

He responded, "If you can't take pleasure in the small and simple things, then what joy could you find in the bigger and more complex things?"

Maggie shrugged her shoulders.

God went on, "A wise man has many vessels in his house. Different vessels serve the many different occasions. Right?"

Maggie answered, "Oh like paper plates, regular porcelain plates, and fine china?"

God replied, "Yes something like that. Well I have mankind, winged creatures, cherubim, seraphim, and arch angels."

Maggie said, "So, we're like paper plates."

God said, "No, because I don't throw you away when I am finished with you. Instead, you are like the clay vessel, breakable but when melted down, you can be remolded. Mankind is the weakest vessel of My collection, but that simply calls for more of My attention, love, and grace."

Maggie watched in awe as God molded and shaped the vessel. He handled it with such care, and attention to detail.

God stopped the wheel and said, "Finished with stage one of sanctification."

As God was getting up to put the clay vessel in the oven to be fired, Maggie stood up and said, "Here, I'll help you."

When she put her hands on the vessel, it flopped over.

Maggie pulled back and said, "Oh I'm so sorry, I was only trying to help and I messed up your art work."

God smiled and said, "Maggie, it's okay I can fix it."

He brought the floppy clay back over to the wheel, and carefully fixed it.

God chucked and stated, "You know, this happens all the time with mankind, they have good intentions, and want to help me fix something or someone."

After putting the clay vessel into the oven, God sat beside Maggie.

He said, "So tell me what's on your mind."

Maggie responded, "Well, Avery was telling me how well Julie was doing, and I am grateful, but I want to see it for myself."

Maggie asked, "Is that possible?"

God answered, "Maggie, honey, anything is possible with God."

Then He scratched his chin and said, "Tell you what, I have an undercover angel stationed at Julie's conference right now, so what I can do is allow you to see through his eyes!"

Maggie jumped up with joy, and hugged God with the tightest squeeze she could muster.

She said, "Thank God, you are so awesome!"

God instructed Maggie to stand facing Him, and then He put His hands over her eyes. When He covered Maggie's eyes, she could see through the eyes of His messenger on earth. The angel was looking at Julie, while she gave a talk to a packed auditorium.

Maggie listened as Julie talked about her experience at Grandview Nursing Home. Julie also spoke about how she believed people suffering with Alzheimer's could still understand everything going on around them. Maggie was so overpowered with joy that the angel she was looking through began to cry.

God removed his hands from Maggie's eyes, and she could see Julie no more.

Maggie hugged God again and said, "Thank you so much for that!"

He replied, "You're very welcome. Don't worry. Julie is in good hands!"

Maggie turned to leave.

God said, "Maggie, your good friend Priscilla is on her way here."

Then He asked, "How would you like to meet her at the gate?"

Maggie replied, "Sure, but only if I can get her back for that nursing home incident with my pinky toe!"

God smiled and said, "All in good fun."

On her way there, Maggie thought about what kind of prank she could pull on Priscilla. When Maggie passed by Charlie's Castle, the perfect idea came to her.

So Maggie walked in and asked, "Charlie, could I borrow Blueberry to pick up Priscilla?"

Charlie answered, "Sure mom, he's in the back. I'll go get him for you."

Charlie flew to the front, and turned Blueberry over to Maggie.

Charlie said, "Have fun!"

Maggie climbed on and said, "Don't worry I will because revenge is sweet!"

And off she went. Upon reaching the pearly gate she saw an angel dropping Priscilla off, so Maggie hopped down from Charlie's horse to greet her.

Priscilla said, "Maggie, I'm here, I'm really here!"

Maggie embraced Priscilla and said, "Just wait until you see Grandma Harrison!"

Priscilla smiled then asked, "What's with the winged blue horse?"

Grinning Maggie said, “Oh that’s our ride, Blueberry!”

Maggie jumped on and helped Priscilla up.

Maggie then shouted, “High ho Blueberry, away!”

Blueberry took off with tremendous speed and power causing Priscilla to shriek.

Maggie giggled like a school girl.

Maggie asked, “Hey Priscilla, do you remember when you dressed up as a doctor to escape Grandview Nursing Home with me as your patient?”

Priscilla nervously answered, “Yes. Why?”

Maggie replied, “Well being that you nearly took off my pinky toe on the way out, I figured that I owed you.”

With that Maggie whispered into Blueberry’s ear, and he suddenly took a dive in an altitude. Then, Blueberry made a hard right diving into a spiral. Maggie giggled the whole way, but Priscilla could only scream and hold on tight.

At last Maggie said, “All right, I think we’re even now!”

And Priscilla responded, “I hope so!”

Maggie landed at Charlie’s castle and they got off.

Maggie asked, “Hey, do you want to meet my son?”

Priscilla said, “Tom?”

Maggie answered, “No, my youngest son

Charlie, who died when he was fourteen."

She said, "Sure."

So they walked across Charlie's draw bridge, and through his door, where he greeted them with a hug. Maggie introduced them.

Priscilla said, "Wow he looks just like you!"

After a short visit Maggie said, "Well we'd best be going, there's still a lot to see!"

So they left Charlie's mansion, and walked along the shoreline of a lake.

They were just catching up, when Priscilla said, "Anything's possible in heaven right?"

Maggie answered, "As far as I know, why?"

Priscilla replied, "Well I have always wanted to swim underwater with the fish like a mermaid!"

They looked at each other and Maggie said, "Why not, it's not like we need oxygen to survive in heaven."

Maggie dove in first, then Priscilla jumped in. Amazingly they were able to swim underwater like mermaids. It was the most beautiful underwater paradise. There were fish of every species, and coral reef like in an ocean. Maggie could see everything perfectly. She wanted to explore further, and discover more of God's creation. She saw the expression of pure bliss on Priscilla's face.

They surfaced, and Priscilla said, "Okay I'm ready to see my mansion now."

After they got out, Priscilla said, "Look

Maggie, we're not even wet!"

Priscilla's remark caused Maggie to remember the dream she had about crossing the stream.

They walked a good way, then reached Priscilla's mansion.

Priscilla shouted with joy, "It's perfect!"

Maggie watched Priscilla run to a massive historical multi-story house that was painted black. Over the black paint were white pok-a-dots all over. Priscilla's mansion was actually trimmed out in fusca pink.

Maggie caught up with Priscilla.

Maggie commented, "It's very much your personality, my dear!"

Priscilla said, "I know, right?"

She turned, and gave Maggie a hug.

Priscilla said, "Thank you so much for praying for me Maggie, you and Grandma Harrison are the reason I'm here."

Maggie responded, "I'd love to take credit, but it belongs to God because He's the one who gave me that dream of you, and God's the one who prompted me to pray for you."

Priscilla asked, "When do I get to meet God face to face?"

Maggie answered, "Soon, but there's still so much to see!"

Moments later Grandma Harrison walked up. Priscilla was so excited that she almost knocked

Maggie over.

Grandma Harrison said, “Well Priscilla, I have been waiting for this moment since you were born.”

Maggie excused herself, and said, “You two have a lot of catching up to do, so I’ll see you later.”

16

WORSHIP SERVICE

Maggie took off down the golden street, but stalled when she realized, that for the first time since getting to Heaven, she was all alone. However, for the first time, in all of Maggie's existence, she did not feel alone.

Maggie looked around heaven, but still hadn't processed all that she had seen. The sound of a trumpet tore through heavens atmosphere with two long blasts. Again, the same two notes blasted through the airwaves, as if to call all of heavens residents to worship.

With every fiber of her being, Maggie felt drawn to the sound that was coming from the throne of God. Maggie made her way closer, and realized that she was not the only one being summoned. The crowd of saints moved in unison, similar to birds flying in groups during migration. The way they moved together was graceful, and never any pushing or shoving.

Maggie thought, “What a call to worship!”

She could finally see where the beautiful sound that summoned them was coming from. The most glorious winged creature held a trumpet to his lips, and he blew a gust of air though a golden instrument.

The angel blew into his horn a final time, then said, “Praise God on High, Father of all creation, and Creator of all things.”

Immediately the focal point changed to the throne of God. In the mist of His throne, Jesus was sitting at the right side of God the Father. The glory of God encompassed His throne, as a rainbow in appearance, and colored like an emerald.

From Maggie’s visual aspect, she saw God surrounded by a bright light. She also could see many beams, of different colored light, shooting out from God. The only comparison Maggie could think of was Earth’s Sun. Some of the colors were like that of a jasper stone.

God’s throne was positioned on a flat surface higher than the rest of the seating. Twenty-four steps flowed from the chancel, on all four sides, to where the crowd gathered. On each corner of the chancel sat a winged creature. The four living creatures had eyes all over their bodies, which enabled them to see in any direction at any time.

The first living creature was like a lion. The second living creature was like a calf. The third living creature had a face like a man, and the fourth creature was like a flying eagle. All four living creatures had six wings, and each wing being full of eyes around and within.

Never resting they chanted over and over again.

The living creatures said, "Holy, Holy, Holy, Lord God Almighty, Who was and is and is to come!"

Further out, but still surrounding God's throne was twenty-four seats. The twenty-four elders who sat on their thrones were clothed in white robes, and wearing crowns of gold. Twelve of the twenty-four elders were the sons of Israel who represented the twelve tribes of Israel. The other twelve of the twenty-four elders were the apostles of the gospel of Christ.

Whenever the four living creatures gave glory and honor to God, who sat on the throne, the twenty-four elders fell down before God to worship Him. They cast their crowns before the throne.

The elders said, "You are worthy, O Lord, to receive glory and honor and power. For you created all things. By your will they exist and were created."

Out of the throne proceeded lightning, thunder, and voices. Standing before the throne of God was seven lamps of fire burning, which were the seven Spirits of God. Beyond the seven spirits of fire was a sea of crystal glass that completely surrounded God's throne. A great multitude, which no one could number, stood on the surface of the crystal sea. Maggie was within the multitude of all nations, tribes, and peoples that stood before the throne and before the Lamb. The great multitude was clothed with white robes, and palm branches in their hands.

They cried out with a loud voice, saying, "Salvation belongs to our God who sits on the throne, and to the Lamb!"

Maggie looked at God, who she had just spoken so casually with.

She thought, "Wow I can't believe God who is so full of majesty, and that rules a whole kingdom would take the time to visit with me, one person!"

Maggie had so much admiration for God. Without saying a word, God's presence exuded Glory, Majesty, Power and Might. On God's right side sat Jesus. Jesus radiated such a glorious kingly flare. The thoughts and emotions that raged through Maggie's being were intense.

Maggie felt, as if she had been given a back stage pass to the most important place ever created. Maggie appreciated the privileged to be apart of this worship service honoring God, but still found it hard to fathom such an important ruler would be interested in the simplicity of her life.

No sooner did Maggie finish that thought, when God stood up, and looked at her.

God said, "Come forward, my child!"

Without any hesitation, Maggie started her journey, and traveled closer to God. Immediately the multitude of people parted, like the red sea. Maggie proceeded to the throne of God.

Maggie reached the bottom step leading up to the throne, and God walked down the remaining twenty-three to meet her. Maggie fell to her knees to worship God, but he grabbed both her hands, and stood her back up.

Maggie still didn't feel worthy enough to look at his face, but God gently lifted her chin.

He said, "Maggie, you are my beloved, and it was the simplicity of your life that I created you for."

Maggie beheld the face of God. She was truly captivated by the amount of love and life in His eyes.

She said, "But I was a nobody on earth, why are you mindful of me?"

God turned his gaze to Jesus, who was still on the throne, and summoned him. Jesus walked down the twenty-four steps.

Jesus replied, "Yes, Lord?"

God said, "Please explain to Maggie why she is of so much value to me."

Jesus looked at Maggie and smiled.

Jesus said, "If you want to be the greatest in the Kingdom of Heaven, then you must be the least of all like the servant. If you want to be first in God's Kingdom, then you must be last in the world."

God said, "Thank you for that explanation."

Maggie hugged both God and Jesus.

She said, "Thank you so much!"

Maggie looked around and asked, "Where's the Holy Spirit?"

God replied, "My Spirit is within us, and all around us."

Jesus looked at God and said, "It's time."

God the Father directed Jesus and Maggie to the front row of those who were gathered for worship. They were facing the throne. Maggie was sort of confused.

She asked, "Why are you in the crowd, and not up on the stage?"

God replied, "Well, I am still the central focus of worship, but this way, everyone in heaven can enjoy the variety of ways in which I am worshiped."

Jesus chimed in and said, "We also like to see, and experience the worship service as you do."

God said, "It's like I am the parent in the audience watching my children perform a talent show that I helped create!"

Maggie was speechless! All around, the lights dimmed. Walking on stage was more than a few electric guitar players. They strung their first cord, and beams of multi-colored lights bounced off the walls of Heaven.

Maggie smiled as she thought, "I feel like I am at a heavy metal concert!"

Growing up Catholic Maggie was taught that anything other than quiet reverence was not tolerated in worship.

Jesus interrupted Maggie's thoughts when he said, "God created all people. He put in their heart, desires that may differentiate vastly. Before this worship service is over, you'll realize just how spicy He truly is."

The next act of worship was a woman with no instrument. The crowd sat down, and an angelic voice came from the women, as she sang of her love to Jesus.

Maggie leaned over to Jesus and whispered, "She must be Church of Christ."

Jesus smiled and nonchalantly said, "Um, Maggie, there are no denominations here."

Next up was a more lively and soulful number. In fact, Maggie felt compelled to stand and dance. Something within the music itself moved the multitude to dance, and sing along with them.

Maggie realized that all of the special music had thoroughly represented every bit of culture behind every nation. Now was the time for God and Jesus to return to their throne.

17

CHRIST'S RETURN

Once seated on His throne, God handed a scroll with seven red wax seals to Jesus.

God announced, "It is time for the second coming."

Jesus stood to his feet. The four living creatures, and the twenty-four elders fell down before Jesus. Each elder had a harp, and golden bowls full of incense, which were the prayers of the saints.

They sang a new song, saying, "You are worthy to take the scroll, and to open its seals because you were slain. You have redeemed us to God by Your blood. Out of every tribe, tongue, people, and nation, You have made us kings, and priests to God. We will reign on the earth."

Then Maggie looked, and heard the voice of more than a million angels around the throne, the living creatures, and the elders chanting.

They all were saying, "Worthy is the Lamb who was slain to receive power, and riches, and wisdom, and strength, and honor, and glory, and blessing!"

At that very moment the walls of heaven disappeared. Everyone in heaven could see all of God's creation from above the boundaries of outer space. Maggie could see all the planets, and stars in the vastness of deep space.

The angels, elders, and the four living creatures stood around the throne. They fell on their faces before the throne, and worshiped God.

They said, "Blessing, and glory, and wisdom, thanks giving, and honor, and power, and might, be to our God forever and ever, Amen."

Jesus opened the first seal. Maggie saw a white horse, and its rider had a bow. A crown was given to him, and he went out conquering, and to conquer.

Jesus opened a second seal, and Maggie saw a fiery red horse. Its rider had a great sword, and it was granted to him to take peace from the earth.

Jesus opened the third seal, and Maggie saw a black horse. Its rider had a pair of scales in his hand to bring famine.

Jesus opened the fourth seal, and Maggie saw a morbidly pale horse. Its rider was the angel of death, and the place of the dead followed him.

Power was given to the four horsemen to kill with a sword, with hunger, with death, and by the beasts of the earth. They were given power and authority over a forth of the earth, in order to cleanse the earth of all wickedness.

Jesus opened the fifth seal, and Maggie saw souls come out from under the altar. They were the souls of those who had been slain for the word of God, and for the testimony which they held. They were those who had died a martyr's death.

They cried out with a loud voice saying, "How long, O Lord, holy and true, until you judge, and avenge our blood on those who dwell on the earth?"

Then a white robe was given to each of them. It was said to them that they should rest a little while longer. Until both the number of their fellow servants and their brethren, who would be killed as they were, was completed.

When Jesus opened the sixth seal, and suddenly there was an earthquake. The sun turned as black as the galaxy surrounding it. The moon turned as red as blood. The stars of heaven fell to the earth, which completely disabled its protective shield causing earth's boundaries to recede as a scroll when it is rolled up.

Every mountain and island was moved out of its place, in order that every hiding place of the wicked was exposed. It was ever clear that God was watching the people's every move, but still the wicked did not repent.

Maggie remembered that Julie and Tom were still on earth, so she walked up to an angel.

She asked, "If my children are still on earth, will they be destroyed?"

The angel looked at Maggie to respond.

The angel said, "They must be believers! However, if they have washed their robes, and made them white in the blood of the Lamb, then they are protected by the seal of God on their foreheads."

Maggie was relieved, and took her place in the multitude. The earth's sky was cracked open, and the top layer was peeled back. The earth's rotation had ceased, and four angels at the four corners of the earth stood holding the four winds of the earth. They did this so that the wind should not blow on the earth, on the sea, or any tree.

Then Maggie saw another angel ascending from the east, having the seal of the living God. That angel cried with a loud voice to the four angels on the four horses, to whom it was granted to harm the earth and the sea.

He shouted, "Do not harm the earth, the sea, or the tree's until we have sealed the servants of our God on their foreheads!"

Jesus opened the seventh seal, and there was silence in heaven for about half an hour. Then Maggie saw the seven angels who stand before God. To them were given seven trumpets. As they prepared themselves to sound, another angel came, and stood at the altar. He had a golden censer, and there was given unto him much incense.

Incense was given to offer it with the prayers of all saints, upon the golden altar, which was before the throne. The smoke of the incense ascended up before God. Mingled in with the smoke were the prayers of the saints.

The angel took the censer, and filled it with fire of the altar. He cast it into the earth, and there were voices, thunder, and lightning, then an earthquake. The golden censer struck the earth, and all of God's creation recognized a battle cry for final destruction.

Afterward, the first angel sounded. Hail and fire, mingled with blood, followed. Fiery hail was thrown to the earth, and a third of the trees were burned up.

The second angel sounded, and something like a great mountain burning with fire was thrown into the sea. A third of the sea became blood, and a third of the living creatures in the sea died. A third of the ships were destroyed.

Then the third angel sounded, and a great star named wormwood fell from heaven. A star burning like a torch fell on a third of the rivers, and on the springs of water. The water became bitter, and caused many men who drank it, to die.

The forth angel sounded. A third of the sun

was struck, a third of the moon, and a third of the stars. So that a third of them were darkened. A third of the day did not shine, and likewise the night.

The fifth angel sounded, and a star fell from heaven to earth. To him was given the key to the bottomless pit. He opened the pit, and smoke arose out of the furnace. So the sun and the air were darkened, because of the smoke of the pit.

Then out of the smoke locust came upon the earth. The locusts were ordered to only harm the people that did not have the seal of God on their foreheads. The locust, also known as demons, had a king over them.

Their king was the angel of the bottomless pit. His name in Hebrew was Abaddon, and in Greek his name was Apollyon, but Maggie recognized him as the serpent of old, the devil.

The sixth angel sounded. A voice sounded from the four horns of the golden altar. The voice spoke to the sixth angel, who had the trumpet.

The voice said, "Release the four angels who are bound at the great river Euphrates."

So the four angels, who had been prepared for the hour, day, month, and year were released to kill a third of the mankind by these three plagues. The three plagues were by fire, smoke, and brimstone. Even after all of this, the rest of mankind still did not repent of the works of their hands, or their wickedness.

The seventh angel sounded and there were

loud voices in heaven.

The voices said, "The kingdoms of this world have become the kingdoms of our Lord, and of His Christ. He will reign forever and ever!"

The anti-Christ rose to power, and deceived all those left on the earth, who had not received the seal of the living God on their foreheads. All those left who were deceived received the mark of the beast on their forehead or their hand.

The mark of the beast was triple six. Most of the saints who had been sealed by God were beheaded for their testimony, and for proclaiming the gospel of Jesus Christ.

Then appeared another sign in heaven. Great and marvelous were seven angels who had the last seven plagues. For in the last seven plagues, the wrath of God is complete.

A loud voice from heaven said to the seven angels, "Go and pour out the bowls of the wrath of God on the earth."

So the first angel went, and poured out his bowl upon the earth. A foul and loathsome sore came upon the men who had the mark of the beast, and those who worshiped his image.

Then the second angel poured out his bowl on the sea, and it became blood as of a dead man. Every living creature in the sea died.

Then the third angel poured out his bowl on the rivers and springs of water, and they became blood.

The angel of the waters said, “You are righteous, O Lord, the One who is and who was and who is to be. You have judged these things, for they have shed the blood of the saints, and prophets. You have given them blood to drink, for it is their just due.”

Another angel from the altar said, “Even so, Lord God Almighty, true and righteous are Your judgements.”

Then the fourth angel poured out his bowl on the sun, and power was given to him to scorch men with fire. Men were scorched with great heat, and they blasphemed the name of God who has power over these plagues. They did not repent and give him glory.

Then the fifth angel poured out his bowl on the throne of the beast, and his kingdom became full of darkness. They gnawed their tongues because of the pain. Again, they blasphemed the God of heaven because of their pains and their sores. Nevertheless, they did not repent of their deeds.

Then the sixth angel poured out his bowl on the great river Euphrates, and its water dried up, so that the way of the kings from the east might be prepared.

Then the seventh angel poured out his bowl into the air, and a loud voice came out of the temple of heaven, from the throne.

The loud voice shouted, “It is done!”

God and Jesus stood up. Maggie could hear a voice coming from the throne.

It said, "Let all people be glad, and rejoice, and give him glory, for the marriage of the Lamb has come, and his wife has made herself ready."

A white horse was presented by an angel to Jesus, who is also called Faithful and True. His eyes were like a flame of fire, and on his head were many crowns. He was clothed with a robe dipped in blood, and his name is called The Word of God. Written on Jesus' robe, and on his thigh is KING OF KINGS AND LORD OF LORDS.

The armies in heaven, clothed in fine linen, white and clean, followed him on white horses. Out of Jesus' mouth came a sharp sword, and with it he should strike the nations. Jesus Himself set out to execute judgment with his words.

All of the birds of the air were summoned to the great feast of flesh, which resulted in Satan's defeat. Maggie was honored to be participating in the second coming of her Lord and Savior. Heaven's residents were trailing behind Jesus.

All the angels of God surrounded Jesus and His saints. Jesus was leading the charge of heaven's army. Upon arrival, Jesus clashed with the beast, his false prophet, and all those who had received his mark.

Maggie witnessed the capture of the beast, and the false prophet. She then joined with the rest of

God's creation, as they shouted in victory. They saw both cast into the lake of fire burning with brimstone. The rest were killed with the sword that proceeded from the mouth of Him who sat on the horse. All the birds were filled with their flesh.

Before Jesus set his foot down on the mount of Olives, all of the living and the dead, the justified and the condemned were caught up to meet Jesus in the air. After the gathering together of all people's, Jesus touched down on the Mount of Olives, and was seated on a white throne.

Furthermore, the sea and hell gave up the dead, and all people were gathered together for the final judgment.

The books of Life were opened, and Jesus began to separate the lost from the saved. Those who were saved by the blood of Christ were put on his right. The condemned, who never accepted Jesus as Lord of their lives but rejected him, were put on his left.

Jesus, The King, addressed those on his right.

He said, "Come, you blessed of My Father. Inherit the kingdom prepared for you from the foundation of the world. For, I was hungry, and you gave me food. I was thirsty, and you gave me drink. I was a stranger, and you took me in. I was naked, and you clothed me. I was sick, and you visited me. I was in prison, and you came to me."

Then the righteous asked, "Lord, when did we

see you hungry and feed you, or naked and cloth you? Or when did we see you sick, or in prison, and come to you?"

Jesus replied, "When you did all these things to the least important of people, because of your love for me, then you did all these things to me."

Then Jesus, The King, announced to those on the left hand.

He said, "Depart from me you cursed, into the everlasting fire prepared for the devil and his angels. For, I was hungry, and you gave me no food. I was thirsty, and you gave me no drink. I was a stranger, and you did not take me in. Sick and in prison, and you did not visit me."

Then the condemned asked, "Lord, when did we see You hungry, or thirsty, or a stranger, or naked, or sick, or in prison, and did not minister to You?"

Jesus answered, "When you refused to do these things in My name and for My glory. Instead, you did these things for your own glory!"

The wicked were cut to the heart for they knew their guilt. They were cast into outer darkness where the worm never dies, and the flame is never quenched.

The righteous in heart was granted eternal life with God Himself. Maggie was finally reunited with Tom and Julie. They lived together happily ever after in God's new Garden of Eden. The old heaven and earth had been brought together and reborn with Jesus

Christ as it's King and Lord.

Acknowledgments

Special thanks, to my family, who provided both encouragement and inspiration for this book. To the churches that we currently serve: St. Matthew's United Methodist Church, Bay Vue United Methodist Church, and Port Bolivar United Methodist Church. The church members of these three churches have supported and encouraged my idea's, and for that I will always be grateful.

I must express gratitude for my husband's help in the creation of this book. Thank you, Marty, for hours of brainstorming, and multiple sessions of proofing. Thanks to Kathy Tucker, Jane Loose, Linda Elissalde, and Butch Kershaw for proofreading and critiquing.

Jean Cripps, who assisted in research regarding dresses of the depression, made from flour and feed sacks. Caroline Akers, Sara Kruft and Sherry Morgan, for moral support.

Finally, to those I have left unnamed, thank you so much for sharing your story, and the emotion that surrounded your tragedy. After all, emotion is the backbone to any good story.

Made in the USA
Charleston, SC
05 September 2014